SHALL WE DANCE?

"You best clean your ears or cut your hair, mister," Evans snarled. "I said vamoose."

With Fargo it was live and let live, but the no-surrender doctrine that emerged in the bloody Republic of Texas era had now spread into Arkansas, Missouri, and the Kansas Territory. It was kill or be killed, no third way. Fargo didn't much like it that way, not being the easy-go killer type. H[ ] rules were the rules, and he was dedic[ ] own survival.

"Tell you what," Fargo replied in a dece[ ] voice. "I'm one to cure a boil by lancing [ ] just decided I might's well kill you and h[ ] with."

Those words, and Fargo's tone, made th[ ] from Evans' face. "Mister, are you a soft[ ] body said nothin' 'bout no killing. Not ye[ ]

Fargo hitched the Ovaro to a tie rail in [ ] saloon. "The killing part came into it,'[ ] plained, facing the man, "when you cal[ ] trash earlier. I don't abide insults, Evans[ ] stranger. You got two choices: swallow [ ] or push daisies."

"You mouthy son of a bitch!" Evan[ ] stepping down into the street. "They'll [ ] in hell afore you'll get an apology. But I [ ] tee you a beatin' you won't forget."

"Then let's open the ball," Fargo invi[ ] ling his heavy leather gun belt.

THE
TRAILSMAN
#296

SIX-GUN
PERSUASION

by

Jon Sharpe

SIGNET
Published by New American Library, a division of
Penguin Group (USA) Inc., 375 Hudson Street,
New York, New York 10014, USA
Penguin Group (Canada), 90 Eglinton Avenue East, Suite 700, Toronto,
Ontario M4P 2Y3, Canada (a division of Pearson Penguin Canada Inc.)
Penguin Books Ltd., 80 Strand, London WC2R 0RL, England
Penguin Ireland, 25 St. Stephen's Green, Dublin 2,
Ireland (a division of Penguin Books Ltd.)
Penguin Group (Australia), 250 Camberwell Road, Camberwell, Victoria 3124,
Australia (a division of Pearson Australia Group Pty. Ltd.)
Penguin Books India Pvt. Ltd., 11 Community Centre, Panchsheel Park,
New Delhi - 110 017, India
Penguin Group (NZ), cnr Airborne and Rosedale Roads, Albany,
Auckland 1310, New Zealand (a division of Pearson New Zealand Ltd.)
Penguin Books (South Africa) (Pty.) Ltd., 24 Sturdee Avenue,
Rosebank, Johannesburg 2196, South Africa

Penguin Books Ltd., Registered Offices:
80 Strand, London WC2R 0RL, England

First published by Signet, an imprint of New American Library,
a division of Penguin Group (USA) Inc.

First Printing, June 2006
10 9 8 7 6 5 4 3 2 1

The first chapter of this book previously appeared in *Oasis of Blood*, the two
hundred ninety-fifth volume in this series.

Copyright © Penguin Group (USA) Inc., 2006
All rights reserved

 REGISTERED TRADEMARK—MARCA REGISTRADA

The Trailsman

Beginnings . . . they bend the tree and they mark the man. Skye Fargo was born when he was eighteen. Terror was his midwife, vengeance his first cry. Killing spawned Skye Fargo, ruthless, cold-blooded murder. Out of the acrid smoke of gunpowder still hanging in the air, he rose, cried out a promise never forgotten.

The Trailsman they began to call him all across the West: searcher, scout, hunter, the man who could see where others only looked, his skills for hire but not his soul, the man who lived each day to the fullest, yet trailed each tomorrow. Skye Fargo, the Trailsman, the seeker who could take the wildness of a land and the wanting of a woman and make them his own.

Northwest Arkansas, 1860—
where murder is epidemic
and Fargo is dispensing the cure—up to six pills per dose.

1

Yet another crackling volley of gunfire echoed through the timbered hill country of northwest Arkansas, reminding the crop-bearded, buckskin-clad rider that the Wild West began almost the moment a man crossed the Mississippi.

Skye Fargo reined in, removing his hat to whack at the flies buzzing around his head. He had spent most of his life desperately trying to avoid the net of civilization, but it was being cast everywhere these days. He patiently studied the surrounding terrain, a patchwork quilt of wooded hills and grassy flats, with the vast Ozark Plateau to the north and mountains visible to the south. He was riding along a narrow divide, the high ground between two valleys.

Fargo's sun-slitted, lake blue eyes were especially vigilant for the glint of rifle barrels. Ragged parcels of cloud drifted across a sky of china blue. It was late summer, with the area deep into a dry spell, and most of the small farmers were running hard just to stand still. The hills, scarred by deep washes, still teemed with sweet clover, though the grass—including crucial pasturage—was yellow-brown from the drought.

"This region's always had its troubles, old campaigner," Fargo remarked quietly to his Ovaro. "But lately, it's become hell turned inside out."

The violence in Arkansas was worse than Fargo had ever seen it. If the Great Plains, beginning just to the west, were the wide front door of the West, then Arkansas was part of the hard threshold. Just to the north the famous westward trails began, at St. Joseph and Independence, Missouri. Arkansas, like Missouri, was a stepping-off place, a lawless borderland with gangs, and even armies, of kill-crazy marauders controlling everyone and everything.

"Well, now, *here's* a tonic," Fargo remarked, perking up and slapping the dust from his buckskins.

A young woman on foot, carrying a sewing basket over one arm, was approaching from behind, headed in the same direction Fargo was riding. Fargo, who sampled women like bees sampled flowers, immediately recognized this gal as a top-shelf sample. A long, fair oval of face peered out from under beribboned russet curls, and perpetually pursed lips egged a man on to kiss them. She wore a pretty, form-flattering dress of sprigged muslin. Nor was this the usual poor hoe-man's daughter—a gold brooch fastened her collar of crocheted lace.

"Hey, long shanks!" she greeted Fargo with a saucy smile. "You get lost from your wagon train? A body can see at a glance you ain't the type to grub taters."

She sashayed past Fargo and stopped in the rutted trail to study him with bold, approving eyes the color of dark berries. Fargo, in turn, leaned forward and rested his muscular forearms on the saddle horn, studying her right back.

"Ain't *you* bold?" she chided without anger as the tall stranger drank her in.

"You can't hang a man for his thoughts," Fargo reminded her.

"Mr. Buckskins, I wouldn't even put *you* on trial," she assured him. "Wild and woolly and hard to curry, I bet. My name, by the way, is Mary Lou Tutt."

"Pleased to meetcha, Mary Lou. The name's Skye Fargo."

"A body don't see fellows of your cut very much around here, Skye," she told him. A shadow crossed her face as a thought occurred to her. "Unless . . . you been sent in to do some killing?"

"From what I can see, Arkansas needs to hire killers like Texas needs to hire prairie dogs."

Even as Fargo fell silent, more gunshots crackled in the distance, making his point.

"It's all because of slavery," Mary Lou said, bitterness edging into her voice. "All a body hears these days is talk about a horrible war coming."

Fargo nodded. The trouble began in earnest with the opening of the Kansas Territory in 1854 and the turbulent question: free or slave? The actual Border War was triggered two years later when fanatical abolitionist John Brown and three of his sons savagely murdered and mutilated five pro-slavery men. With talk of a great civil war now brewing, the battle had become the Kansas abolitionists or Jayhawkers, "Free Staters," versus the Missouri "Border Ruffians," pro-slavers.

Both sides used the slavery issue as an excuse to kill and plunder. Arkansas got sucked into the mess by virtue of its crucial location and high number of caves. Pro-slavery gangs, often drunk, patrolled the country, harassing all would-be settlers. Not surprisingly, new arrivals formed their own militia bands for self-defense—and now armed bands were everywhere, thick as ticks on a hound.

"It's got so confused," Fargo told Mary Lou, "that troops sent in to restore order end up fighting both factions. Up in Kansas, the new governor just resigned in outright fear for his life. Hell, on my way here I saw at least a thousand Border Ruffians encamped on the Missouri-Arkansas line. The U.S. Army couldn't muster even half that number out here—not with war building back east."

"Pukes," Mary Lou said, her voice harsh with contempt as she used the popular name for the Border Ruffians. "Puttin' colored folks in chains and callin' themselves Christians. It's a sin to Moses."

However, Fargo noticed a glint of sudden suspicion in those berry-juice eyes. "Skye, you seem to know plenty about the army and such. Is that why you're here—sent in by the army for a look-see?"

Fargo laughed, strong white teeth flashing through his beard. "You sure are a *wary* lass," he teased her. "What's a pretty young thing like you so afraid of?"

"If you lived around here, you'd know."

"Well, you can rest easy about me. I sometimes work for the army, sure, but only as a civilian contract scout. Matter fact, I just finished three months work out in the Far West for the War Department's Corps of Topographical Engineers."

"Topo-*who*?" she cut in. "Laws, that's a mouthful."

"Mapmakers," he explained, grinning. "We mapped the Black Rock Desert in northern Utah Territory and parts of the Humboldt River country."

"That's sure a far piece from Arkansas," she reminded him.

"I'm here because, after my contract expired, I came across a small party of emigrants from west Tennessee. They'd been attacked by Comanches in New Mexico Territory, half of them killed or wounded. The survivors wanted no part of the West and begged me to guide them back home. There were several kids along, so I took everybody back to Tennessee. Now my needle points west again. I'm headed toward Pikes Peak country."

The suspicion eased from Mary Lou's face and was replaced by disappointment. "So you won't be staying in Lead Hill very long?" she asked, her tone urging him to reconsider.

"Lead Hill?" he repeated. "Not a very reassuring name. Never heard of it."

Again a pensive frown transformed her pretty face. "Oh, it's aptly named, for a surety. Lies straight ahead about two miles. Place ain't been there long, though."

Fargo wasn't surprised. Jerkwater towns were springing up all over this part of the West—so called because many of them were water stops where the train crews jerked a chain to lower the waterspout over the boiler.

"Lead Hill got a livery or a blacksmith?" Fargo asked her.

She nodded. "Romer Wiltz runs both."

Fargo was in a pinch. He had foolishly trusted a drunken blacksmith back in Batesville, and now his stallion's right rear shoe had been clicking for several miles. Bad shoeing lamed more horses than anything else, and unless the shoe was pulled and reset immediately, the pinto would almost surely founder—and Fargo's hasp and shoeing hammer had been stolen from his saddlebags in Tennessee.

"I require the services of this Romer Wiltz," Fargo told Mary Lou. "How 'bout you, pretty lady? Headed to town?"

"Ain't exactly a town, but sure, I'm headed there to leave some work for the seamstress. And I *do* ride horseback in a dress, case you're offering to take me."

"Be glad to . . . take you," Fargo punned with a sly grin, swinging down to help this tasty little country tidbit into the saddle.

"Glad? Oh, I guarantee you'd be powerful glad, Mr. Buckskins," she promised in a voice gone husky. "So why'n't you stay around awhile?"

4

Fargo hadn't done the mazy waltz in weeks, and this Arkansas beauty was definitely a suitable nubile prospect. Her frank talk already had him aroused. He swung her up into leather, pleasantly aware of her ample breasts pressuring his back, her moist, warm breath on his neck.

They had barely gotten under way, Fargo holding the Ovaro to an easy trot, when the rataplan of racing hooves approached from behind. Fargo sent a cross-shoulder glance to the rear and saw a coal black stallion racing toward them, his rider whipping him to a lather with a leather quirt.

"Oh, Moses on the mountain!" Mary Lou fretted, her grip on Fargo's midsection tightening in fear. "Skye, I am *so* sorry!"

"Why? That your husband or beau?"

"Huh! Neither one. That's Clay Evans coming, and he's a mite tetched—his whole clan is. You might say he's set his cap for me—his *night*cap. But he means to kill me after he rapes me."

Fargo had more questions, but right now he had to get set for possible trouble. He reined right, clearing the trail for Clay Evans, and then knocked the riding thong off the hammer of his belt gun. He left his palm resting on the butt of the Colt, but didn't clear leather. It was as volatile here as anywhere else in the West, and a man had to be very careful about filling his hand. Fargo had seen too many pissing fights end in a coil of blue gun smoke.

However, the rider never even slackened his pace. Fargo glimpsed a strapping, hatless young man in his early twenties, with a round, flushed face and hair black as licorice, slicked back with axle grease. Many young men of this turbulent area were not considered criminals, but rather, "harum-scarum"—reckless and unpredictable. The look in this man's eyes, however, when they met Fargo's, was unmistakably murderous.

The moment Clay Evans switched his reins to his left hand, freeing his gun hand, Fargo skinned out his Colt quicker than eyesight. Since Evans hadn't actually drawn, Fargo merely held the shooter ready for action, but not aimed.

For a moment Evans stared in disbelief, perhaps wondering how that gun got into Fargo's fist so rapidly. Whatever he'd planned, he again took the reins in both hands. Now his attention shifted to Mary Lou.

"Two-bit whore!" he insulted her as he thundered past. He included Fargo in the insult when he added, "I see you hump trail trash now! Got tired of Injins and darkies, huh?"

"Murdering scum!" she threw after him. "Killed a child today?"

"Oh, Jesus," Fargo said, figuring out the clues. "The Tutts and the Evanses are feuding, right?"

"You just keep your nose out of the pie," she snapped, still seething with anger. "And be mighty careful, hear? Now he's seen you with me, he'll be down on you like all wrath."

"His choice," Fargo said calmly, sliding the thong over the hammer and kneeing the Ovaro forward. That "trail trash" remark had been duly noted and filed away. "I'll be having a little discussion with him, I expect."

"Skye, don't you dare! You'll catch a weasel asleep before you ever talk any sense into that no-account Evans trash."

"His choice," Fargo said again. "Me, I'm a lovable cuss. That's it, darlin'. Hang on tight."

"Like this, Skye? Or is my left hand too low?"

An ear-to-ear smile divided Fargo's bearded, weather-bronzed face. "*Just* like that, Miss Mary Lou."

2

Only a quarter-mile after he met Mary Lou, Fargo spotted a water hole just off the trail. He rode past it when he noticed the willow trees around it were stunted—water where willows and cottonwoods refused to grow was bad.

Just beyond, however, was a trickle too thin to call a creek, but good water just the same.

Fargo drew rein, carefully helped Mary Lou light down, then threw off and filled his canteens before dropping the stallion's bridle and watering him.

"Why bother watering here?" Mary Lou asked. "Lead Hill ain't but a stone's throw away. Romer's got a big tank of free water in front of his livery."

"When I ride into a new town," Fargo replied, "I like to be ready to ride *out* in a puffin' hurry."

"If you're a bank robber, Skye, Lead Hill ain't got none—banks, I mean."

Fargo laughed. "I'm no scrubbed angel, Mary Lou, but bank heists are a mite out of my line."

They were back in the saddle, the tree-lined trail winding higher now and giving Fargo a panoramic view of hilly terrain for miles around. This area was honeycombed with caves and dotted with steep river bluffs. Arkansas, he reflected, was not nearly so rugged as the black lava canyons of the Snake River, nor so breathtaking as the Yellowstone country. But easy game was plentiful: he'd seen ducks and geese near the rivers, deer, rabbits, and quail in the thickets.

"Where was Clay Evans headed in such an all-fired hurry?" Fargo asked his passenger.

"Oh, them Evans men got plenty of irons in the fire," Mary Lou replied, her voice brittle with sarcasm. "All of 'em bloody and dirty. Langston, Clay's pa, is thick as thieves with that Border Ruffian bunch, and so is Clay and his younger brother, Dobie. They got a cousin named Scooter lives with 'em, *that* boy is savage as a meat ax. Two weeks ago I saw him beat a horse to death with his bare fists, my hand to God."

"Sound like some unpleasant fellows," Fargo agreed.

"They certainly are, and Clay considers himself the big he-dog hereabouts," Mary Lou warned. "Just now he looked shooting mad, so you best take care, Mr. Buckskins. Course, you don't strike me as the flighty type."

"Tell me," Fargo pressed, "how long has this Tutt-Evans feud been fought?"

"What 'feud'?" she reproached him. "You *are* notional. Some things are best left alone."

7

Fargo dropped the subject, but feuds, in this region populated by mountain people from Tennessee and Kentucky, were numerous and often bloody. Rarely did the law step in.

The trail wound free of the dense tree cover, and Fargo got his first look at Lead Hill, Arkansas, a dusty crossroads settlement erected in the grassy lee of a small hill. There was only one street, wide and dusty, and a handful of businesses, most built of mud-chinked logs or raw slab lumber. The settlement pattern of family dwellings aped the South, with single-room log cabins nestled among tree stumps. Larger dwellings were made from two cabins connected by a dogtrot or breezeway. Several flea-bitten hounds lay in the shade, too lazy to bark at new arrivals.

"Oh, lands," Mary Lou muttered. "That's Clay standing in front of the saloon. And he's laying for you, Skye."

"Don't worry, I tend to draw these rough, unsavory types," Fargo remarked cheerfully. "Where you going, Mary Lou?"

"There," she said, pointing to a cabin with a "fashion baby" in the window, a doll sent over from Europe dressed in a miniature of the latest Parisian gown. "Holly Nearhood's place. She's makin' me a gown just like that one in the window. Now you be careful, Skye, Clay is a dirty fighter. He won't likely kill you in town, not in broad daylight with witnesses. But he's good with a knife, and he likes to cripple men by slicing their tendons."

Fargo handed her down and continued on toward a combination harness shop, feed stable, and blacksmith's forge. As he drew abreast of the ramshackle Three Sisters saloon, a voice sharp with authority accosted him.

"Safety tip, mister. Hit the breeze, and hit it quick."

Fargo reined in and stared at Clay Evans, getting a better size-up of him. He took in the fancy calfskin boots with two-inch heels, the fancy brocaded vest. He wore two ivory-handled .36 caliber Colt Navy revolvers, model 1851, in rawhide holsters. General opinion in the West held that a man could wear one revolver, or none, but two marked either a grandstander or a killer.

"You best clean your ears or cut your hair, mister," Evans snarled. "I said vamoose."

With Fargo it was live and let live, but the no-surrender doctrine that emerged in the bloody Republic of Texas era had now spread into Arkansas, Missouri, and the Kansas Territory. It was kill or be killed, no third way. Fargo didn't much like it that way, not being the easy-go killer type. However, the rules were the rules, and he was dedicated to his own survival.

"Tell you what," Fargo replied in a deceptively soft voice. "I'm one to cure a boil by lancing it. And I've just decided I might's well kill you and have it done with."

These words, and Fargo's conversational tone, made the color ebb from Evans' face. "Mister, are you a soft-brain? Nobody said nothin' 'bout no killing. Not yet, anyhow."

Fargo swung down and hitched the Ovaro to a tie rail in front of the saloon. "The killing part came into it," Fargo explained, facing his man, "when you called me trail trash earlier. I don't abide insults, Evans, not from a stranger. Now you got two choices: swallow back those words or push daisies."

"You mouthy son of a bitch!" Evans exploded, stepping down into the street. "The goddamn gall. They'll get holidays in hell afore you'll get an apology from me. But I *will* guarantee you a beatin' you won't forget."

"Then let's open the ball," Fargo invited, unbuckling his heavy leather gun belt.

An expression of loutish cunning twisted Clay's face as he, too, dropped his gun belt. "Stranger, you picked the wrong place to start feelin' frisky. You *coulda* rode outta here in one piece, Jayhawker. Now I'm fixin' to pound you into paste."

Fargo could understand the thug's confidence. Clay Evans was a man mountain, solid muscle and at least two inches taller than Fargo and heavier in build. As he moved in on Fargo, massive fists doubled, he taunted his adversary. "Your whore is watchin' us right now, Jayhawker trash. I hope you already got some a her quim 'cause she's about to see her struttin' rooster turned into a capon. You—*unh!*"

Fargo, showing no flash and little legwork, set his heels and straight-armed Evans in the mouth, then waded relentlessly closer and slammed his head with repeated right and left crosses. With the big man reeling, Fargo sailed in a haymaker that picked Evans up off the ground and then dropped him smack on his ass, spitting out blood and tooth fragments.

"Two choices," Fargo reminded the dazed man. "Apologize or I'll thrash you into the grave."

"Eat shit, cock chafer! You coldcocked me. That ain't fair!"

That was another lie, as was Evans' accusation that Fargo was a Jayhawker, a member of the region's far-flung abolitionist guerrillas who were themselves as criminal as the Border Ruffians.

"Then stand up," Fargo growled. "You got some manners to learn, boy, even if it kills you."

Evans, nearly out of breath from fury and exertion, heaved himself to his feet and, snarling savagely, charged Fargo, his head down like a bull. The Trailsman knew that most fistfights ended up on the ground, turning into wrestling matches. Against a strapping bear like Clay Evans, however, that was a fool's play.

Fargo couldn't get out of the raging bull's way, so instead he gave way in the direction of the charge, encircling his crouched opponent with both arms. Fargo rolled onto his back hard and fast, Evans' own momentum sending him sprawling into the dust.

"Live to bounce your grandkids on your knee, Evans," Fargo suggested. "Apologize."

"Bounce a cat's tail, you son of a bitch!" This time, when Evans scrambled to his feet, there was a wicked-looking bowie knife in his right hand. "You're goin' up, mister, bank on it!"

Mary Lou's warning came back to Fargo: *he likes to cripple men by slicing their tendons.*

"You cowards always change the rules when you're losing," Fargo said. "Never fails. Well, if it's blades you're partial to . . ."

Like most men full of themselves, Evans was a poor observer of details, and he had failed to notice Fargo's boot sheath. However, he took close notice when the Arkansas toothpick appeared in Fargo's hand. A bowie was deadly, but the toothpick's long, narrow blade was designed for efficient killing. Nor did Evans fail to notice how expertly Fargo shifted it from hand to hand.

"Let's put a ribbon on this, boy," Fargo said. "Now it's down to the killing."

Evidently, Clay Evans had just realized this, too, judging by the way his face looked as if he'd just been leeched. Fargo recalled Mary Lou saying Clay was handy with a knife, but obviously he was nerve-rattled by this bearded stranger who coolly, methodically imposed his unbending will. He held back, his face unsure as he eyed Fargo's frog-sticker.

"You're a paid killer," Evans stated as if it were a fact. "Sent by the Jayhawker trash, right?"

"Close for the kill or apologize, two-gun man," Fargo snapped. "It's hot in this sun."

Fargo saw Evans' gimlet eyes flick down the street, where Mary Lou stood watching. Several other locals peered out from shaded doorways. Evans looked truly miserable as he made up his mind.

"All right, stranger," he surrendered. "I apologize for what I called you back on the trail."

Fargo nodded, saying nothing. He never humiliated a defeated opponent nor gloated in victory. However, he could tell from the homicidal rage in Evans' face that the matter was far from over.

Fargo buckled on his gun, keeping a wary eye to all sides, and then led the Ovaro toward the sprawling livery barn at the edge of the settlement.

He washed up at the trough in front of the barn and led his black-and-white pinto into the hay-scented interior of the barn. A short, strong forge man built like a barrel was warping a tire around a wheel. He wore homespun clothing and old, heavy work boots with welt stitching.

"I'm guessing you must be Romer Wiltz," Fargo greeted him. "Got time to reset a shoe?"

"No, but I'll *make* time."

Wiltz left the bellows and crossed the barn. When he offered to shake with Fargo, the Trailsman saw how his hands were permanently crippled from hard work.

"I just have to shake your paw, stranger," the blacksmith explained. "It was a pure-dee pleasure to watch you whale the tar out of Clay Evans just now. You shoulda killed him, though. Them Evans men nurse a grudge until it hollers mama."

Fargo nodded. "Some of these young bucks got more muscle than good sense."

"No, that's sugarcoating it. Stranger, you're the kind any man would be proud to ride the river with. But there's only one of you, and the Evans clan is spread throughout the surrounding hills. Light a shuck outta here, and don't stop till you're days away."

"Prob'ly good advice," Fargo agreed, knowing his own contrary nature—he'd likely ignore it.

Romer fished a plug of black shag from his pocket and cut a chaw off it. When he had it cheeked and juicing good, he said, "That pert-lookin' gal you was sweet-talkin' is Mary Lou Tutt. Her clan and the Evanses been feudin' these past years."

"Over what?"

Wiltz shrugged. "Hell, is there ever a good reason? Anyhow, Clay is hot in rut for Mary Lou even though he hates her. I was you, I wouldn't come 'tween *that* dog and his meat."

"If you had to take sides," Fargo said, "which clan would you back?"

"The Tutts," Romer replied without hesitation. "Sure, Joshua Tutt, Mary Lou's pa, is a cantankerous old flint, though now he's soft in the head from a horse kick. They're hardworking farmers. Use to, both clans was spread through these northern hills. So far, though, twenty total been killed, Tutts and Evanses, and they're on the verge of wiping each other out."

Wiltz ran a hand over the Ovaro's impressive musculature. "Fine-looking animal," he praised. "Whatever you do, mister, keep this stallion in sight at all times until you've at least passed Eureka Springs west of here."

Fargo, busy stripping the Ovaro of tack, asked why.

Wiltz glanced nervously toward the wide double doors. "Because the Evans clan are just flat-out horse thieves. In a big way. They supply mounts to the Border Ruffians. And there ain't been horseflesh like yours in Lead Hill since God was a boy."

"Much obliged for the warning," Fargo told him. He tossed his saddle onto a rack in the tack room and hung his bridle from a coffee can nailed to the wall.

The doors swung open, creaking like coffin lids, and a

figure was backlit by the furnace-hot sun. Fargo knocked the thong from the Colt's hammer and palmed the butt. However, it was only an elderly customer picking up a mended harness. Romer Wiltz didn't bat an eye when the man paid with a handful of new nails. Out west nails were so scarce, and so badly needed, that most folks heading west burned down their old homes to recover them.

While Romer pulled and reset the Ovaro's right rear shoe, Fargo curried the dried sweat off the stallion and gave him a brisk rubdown with a feed sack. A good feed of oats and crushed barley, and the Ovaro was back in fine fettle.

Romer refused to take any money, insisting it was a rare privilege to watch any man set Clay Evans on his ass hard. Fargo, leading his horse, stepped out into the glaring sunshine and immediately heard the menacing click of a hammer being cocked.

"Unbuckle that gun belt, mister," ordered an authoritative voice. "And do it slow, or I'll get nervous and shoot before I think."

The man standing in the shadow of the building looked to be about fifty years old and wore a six-pointed star on his rawhide vest. His Smith & Wesson repeater was leveled on Fargo.

"You're the sheriff?" Fargo asked—around here appearances meant nothing.

"Sheriff Hollis Maitland, duly elected. Now drop that gun belt, and drop it slow."

"I'm gonna do it so slow," Fargo assured him, "that it won't get done."

Maitland thumbed the hammer to full cock. "Either that smoke wagon hits the dirt or you do."

"If this is about the fight just now," Fargo said, "what laws were broken?"

"I saw the fight, and Clay Evans had no call to jump you. But we got a local law here, mister. Locals can go heeled, but vagrants, drunks, and drifters are prohibited from carrying weapons. You check your guns when you ride in, pick 'em up when you leave."

Fargo's smile was toothy and a little menacing. "Well, I've got money, I'm sober, and I know my destination, which means I'm not drifting."

"Sorry, son." The sheriff wagged his six-gun for emphasis. "We also got us a rash of sneak-thievery in the area, and any new face is cause for suspicion. I've got to disarm you."

Fargo shook his head. "It's all right to take a man's gun in New York or Philadelphia, but this is the frontier—and just as wild as any other part of the West. I b'lieve I'll be keeping my weapons."

Quicker than thought, Fargo's Colt leaped into his fist and spat orange muzzle streak. The gun flew from Sheriff Maitland's uninjured right hand. Fargo immediately leathered his Colt.

"By the horn spoons!" the sheriff said, realizing he'd overstepped. "Mister, that was some serious shooting. I've just decided I'm done trying to disarm you. For thirty dollars a month I've done my duty. 'Sides, *you* ain't no outlaw—I've seen enough to know their look and swagger."

"Obliged," Fargo told him as the sheriff picked up his gun and sauntered off, trying not to look humiliated.

Romer Wiltz appeared in the doorway behind Fargo. "More good work, fella. But don't let old Hollis honeyfuggle you. They say there's no law west of Arkansas. Truth is, there ain't none here, either. Hollis was put up and elected by the Evans clan. Oh, he ain't a killer, but he knows which side his bread is buttered on. And he never loses a wink of sleep over another dead body in the street. Matter fact, Lead Hill has never even had a murder trial."

Fargo already knew all that about this region. As in the frontier beyond the hundredth meridian, the wholesale killings were rarely investigated—even if reported. Killing, in the West, did not carry the stigma it did back east. Even when an obviously guilty man was arrested, he was often acquitted or given a short prison sentence.

"Skye!"

Fargo was surprised to see Mary Lou hurrying toward him, basket swinging on her arm. She must have stayed outside the entire time.

"Skye, you're in a passel of trouble now," she reproached him. "You fight like a bobcat unleashed, but you made a humdinger of a mistake by not killing Clay Evans. That man is prideful, and you gelded him right in front of me. He'll never let you live."

"Story of my life," Fargo replied, cinching his latigos. "I'm just a lovable cuss who minds his own halter. But somehow I always end up in the crosshairs."

"Well, just in case you'd like to *prove* just how lovable you are," she teased, aiming an entreating glance at him, "why not give me a ride home? See, there's this nice, private little spot where we could . . . visit for a while."

Fargo was a man of iron discipline, used to strict self-denial when required, but he rarely turned down a willing female. Older, younger, blondes, redheads, preachers' daughters or soiled doves, plump girls or skinny—once they sent him the go sign, he was happy to wrinkle their sheets.

"A visit sounds real nice," the Trailsman agreed, helping her into the saddle.

However, even as he stepped into leather and swung up and over, thumping the Ovaro's ribs with his heels, Fargo wondered where the hell Clay Evans had disappeared to.

3

"Ain't but a short way now," Mary Lou said, her breath tickling Fargo's ear. "The place is about a mile before you get to our farm. Found it when I was a bitty girl."

They were riding along a valley floor, following an iron-rutted road. During droughts malaria ravaged the lowlands, and Fargo saw white towels tied to yard gates to warn off strangers.

"Pa says land and crop values is low," Mary Lou told him, watching Fargo survey everything. "Two years of drought, plus everybody leavin' to dig for gold out on the Comstock or at Pikes Peak. 'Zif that ain't bad enough, these blamed Pukes got everybody scairt to settle here."

No question, Fargo realized, that northern Arkansas, like Kansas and Missouri, had become a boiling cauldron because of the free-soil versus slaver battle. However, neither side cared much about the fate of the Negro—the slavery question was merely an excuse to burn and pillage.

"Speaking of gold," Mary Lou said, pointing toward a nearly dry streambed on their right. Fargo wasn't surprised to see about a dozen farmers and laborers intently studying the streambed. Farther west, the annual summer drought shrank the streams, exposing the bars of gold-rich ground. These folks were hoping for the same luck.

"What do you know about Hollis Maitland?" Fargo asked her.

"He's a badge-happy bully who's on the Evans payroll, I know *that* much. He was fixin' to kill you, Skye, so he could hold a sheriff's auction. That Evans bunch woulda got your fine horse for mebbe ten dollars, sold it for five hundred."

Fargo had forgotten about sheriff's sales. By custom, when a stranger was killed in a small town, his horse and other possessions were auctioned off to pay for his burial.

"Romer Wiltz said the sheriff isn't a murderer," he pointed out.

"Well . . . I don't know certain-sure of anybody he's murdered," Mary Lou conceded. "But he takes money from them as does kill. Likely, Hollis would be middling honest if Langston Evans hadn't bullied him into licking his boots. How 'bout you, Mr. Buckskins? You like workin' for the army?"

"Not generally," Fargo admitted. "Especially when it's a mapmaking expedition."

"Well? Don't folks need maps?"

"Folks need coffins, too, don't they?"

Fargo left it at that. He had always felt guilty about guiding topographical crews into virgin wilderness. After all, the point of these new maps was to give westward-bound emigrants reliable information about distances, campsites, river fords, grazing conditions and mountain passes—in other words, to help the pilgrims overrun him. At least he had the consolation of knowing those maps helped save hundreds of lives.

"Won't be long now," Mary Lou breathed in his ear, her hot, moist tongue giving him a tickling lick. "Just around the bend where that old gristmill sets."

Fargo had not rested easy since riding out of Lead Hill with no idea where Clay Evans went. He reined in and sent his eyes searching in every direction. The Ovaro, usually an excellent sentry, was the victim of biting horseflies and was busy stamping his forefeet and swinging his long mane to drive them off. Fargo had to trust his own senses.

"Worried about Clay Evans?" Mary Lou asked.

"Shouldn't I be?"

"You better be," she said passionately. "Since I been old enough for men to want to bed me, that man has plagued me most to death. He'll rape and kill me, he's promised me that."

A moment later Mary Lou loosed a titter. "He *did* look mighty puny feelin', though, after you thrashed him, Skye. Still, you best clear out of here soon."

When Fargo said nothing to this, Mary Lou added, "Best to study on it, Skye. Ain't just Clay you locked horns with—it's the whole Evans clan."

They rounded a shady bend and the stone gristmill receded behind tree cover.

"Just ahead now," Mary Lou promised, one hand dropping lower to explore inside the fly of Fargo's buckskin trousers. At the first intimate caress, his member went rigid as a flagpole. Mary Lou sucked in a surprised, delighted breath.

"Holy Hannah! Now *there's* an organ big enough to play in any cathedral. Hurry, Skye, oh, *hurry!*"

Her sudden and powerful arousal ignited Fargo's own. She touched his arm when it was time to angle off the trail into a private, well-hidden plum thicket near a small creek. A bracken of ferns formed a private inner chamber, with pine boughs for a soft bed.

Fargo helped Mary Lou down and then pulled his Henry from its boot. Just then, above the steady crackle of insects, he heard a familiar sound: the thundering of hooves, scores of them.

"That's trouble if they're riding our way," Fargo remarked, kneeling to feel the ground with three fingertips.

"They ain't," Mary Lou said confidently.

"You're right," Fargo said, watching her from narrowed eyes. "The vibrations are getting weaker. How'd you know?"

At first Mary Lou's pretty face closed like a vault door. "There's things us Tutts don't discuss with outlanders."

"Outlander?" Fargo grinned. "Clay Evans just tried to skin me, and you've brought me to your secret place. Hell, I'm prac'ly a neighbor."

Mary Lou relented. "Them horses you hear, Skye, are Pukes comin' back from a raid or a crime or some such. The Missouri border ain't but a few miles from here. You ever heard of Devil's Mouth?"

Fargo, busy unbuckling his heavy gun belt, shook his head.

"It's a cave—anyhow, s'posed to be a cave—hidden somewheres on Langston Evans' property. *Big* cave with freshwater and an escape tunnel. Langston and his no-'count boys steal horses and sell 'em to the Border Ruffians. He also lets them use Devil's Mouth to hide in after a killing spree. That's where them horses was headed—into the cave."

"Pretty serious charge," Fargo said. "Then again, there's thousands of caves in Missouri and plenty in Arkansas. If you've got proof, it should be reported to the army at Fort Smith."

Mary Lou, who struck Fargo as the fanciful type, sat down on the pine boughs and began removing her side-lacing shoes. "Us Tutts don't bring law into our fights. Skye, have you ever heard of Persephone?"

"It's a spice, innit?"

"A *spice*?" Her laughter was musical. "No, goose! Persephone was this beautiful goddess in the way-back days. See, she was abducted by Pluto, god of the underworld, and taken to Hades—that's hell."

By now Mary Lou had her shoes off and was shucking out of her ruffled pantaloons. "Sometimes," she added, "I think that's going to happen to me. Only, Pluto will be Clay Evans, and Hades will be Devil's Mouth. But, here, have a look—I'm ready for some fun."

She pulled her dress and chemise up to her hips and spread those long, shapely legs wide open. The pink petals and folds of her sex were honey glazed with desire and radiated the damp-earth odor of female arousal.

"You like?" she asked him.

"Better than a gold mine," he assured her.

Mary Lou's smile was vain. "Better than any other gal you'll find around here. It gets mighty boresome of a night in these parts, and I gave it away for free before I realized I could move to a city and barter with it. But a fella like you, *I'd* pay."

"Now there's wages a man can live with."

"Think you can scratch my itch, Mr. Buckskins?" she teased him, scooting her butt around in her eagerness.

Fargo leaned the Henry against a tree. "Let's probe the issue," he suggested. "See if we can't get to the bottom of it."

Mary Lou had already handled his impressive male endowment. When Fargo dropped his trousers and she actually saw it, however, she stared like a bird mesmerized by a snake.

"That gorgeous thing will be in the next county hours before you are," she marveled. "Let Mary Lou give it a little kiss."

Her "little kiss" turned into countless minutes of pleasure for Fargo. Her tongue studied his curved saber like a curious finger. She took slow and lingering licks one moment, ravenous tastes the next.

"Honey," Fargo warned reluctantly, "if you want the first one to go inside you, you better stop—uhh, you better—hell, don't you dare stop!"

Mary Lou had no such damn fool notion. She had both of them fired up like train boilers. The huge part of him that didn't fit in her mouth she stroked fast in a tight fist. Her free left hand gripped his wrinkled sac, squeezing gently while her lips, tongue, and teeth played his shaft like a wind instrument.

Fargo felt the pleasure build into a tight, insistent pressure in his groin that spread in radiating waves that soon had his entire body twitching.

"*Give* it to me, Mr. Buckskins!" she cried, mumbling around his steel-hard erection. "*Now*, you randy stallion!"

Fargo groaned deeply, arched his back hard, and spent himself in repeated releases that left after tremors in his belly and groin.

Even as he felt himself slipping into a post-release daze,

however, Fargo thought he heard the Ovaro softly nicker. *Check that out, Fargo*, the survivor in him urged. Moments later the sexually satisfied Fargo drifted into a light sleep.

A hand touched Fargo's shoulder, nudging him out of his doze, and before his eyes even opened his Arkansas toothpick was in his hand.

A feminine titter brought him fully awake. "Laws, Skye! Now it's *my* turn to get some pleasurin', but that's not the kinda pokin' I had in mind."

Her hand moved to his newly aroused member. "Don't take you long to recharge that weapon, does it?"

Fargo gazed at the furry nest between her legs. Her inner thighs were shiny from her arousal. "Not when the hunting is so good. Let's take care of this."

However, even as Fargo fitted himself into his favorite saddle he remembered the Ovaro nickering from his position outside the bracken of ferns. There had been no more warnings since then, but Fargo still felt it—a premonition in his primitive nerves, not his brain.

"Damn," he cursed, rolling off Mary Lou, "give me just a minute to check—"

Fargo never finished his sentence. Outside their little shelter, on the nearby trail, someone unleashed a shrill laugh. "Hey, Mary Lou! I seen you suckin' his one-eyed worm, you abolitionist whore!"

"Dobie Evans!" Mary Lou exclaimed, sitting up in fright. "Clay's kid brother. We're in trouble, Skye."

Fargo, caught with his pants down once again, had already figured that out. He sprang to his feet and hefted his rifle. A heartbeat later, the hot, lazy afternoon erupted in violent gunfire.

Fargo hadn't even cocked the Henry before a hail of lead tore into the thicket, shredding leaves, chipping bark and hornet-buzzing past his ears. He thought about the Ovaro, partially exposed to the trail, but at least two men were firing repeating rifles full bore, and at the moment Fargo had no choice but to get out of the weather.

Mary Lou screamed like a banshee and made the stupid mistake of standing up. Fargo tackled her and kept her covered with his body until the rifle fire began to slacken.

Just then the Ovaro whickered in anger, men cursed

nearby, and a whip began cracking viciously. The desperate neighing of his stallion laid a chill on Fargo.

"The barn rats're stealing my horse," Fargo said, grabbing his Colt and thumb-cocking it. His problem was visibility—Fargo dared not open fire from a blind position for fear of hitting his stallion. When he attempted to emerge from the bracken of ferns, however, hot lead pushed him back.

More angry whickers, more whip cracks, and finally the racket moved out onto the trail. A rapid thunder of hooves marked the thieves' escape, reluctant Ovaro in tow.

By the time Fargo reached the trail, the two thieves were racing full chisel toward the hills. He levered a round into the Henry's chamber and swung the stock up into his shoulder socket. The Henry was not a powerful knockdown gun like the Sharps or the Hawken, but its accuracy, reliability, and sixteen-shot magazine more than made up for its modest caliber.

"Shit," Fargo muttered, lowering the muzzle. "The way they're bent low in the saddle, I'll hit my horse instead of them."

"That's Clay Evans' brother Dobie and their disgusting cousin Scooter," Mary Lou supplied. "Scratch an Evans, you'll find a horse thief."

The escaping thieves were still well in sight when the rataplan of more hooves approached from behind Fargo.

"Christ, the roaches are coming out of the woodwork," he said, watching a rider on a strawberry roan flying toward them like the 2:20 express. Fargo started to aim the Henry.

"Don't shoot!" Mary Lou cried. "That's my brother Baylor."

"He's wasting his time," Fargo remarked as Baylor flashed past, hunched low over his pommel. "Even if he can catch them, he'll face a storm of lead."

"Not Baylor," Mary Lou said confidently. "He spent two years down in the Live Oak country of deep Texas, catching wild horses. Learned tricks from the Mexican cowboys. Watch this."

Fargo recognized the bolas Tutt had begun to swing in a circle over his head: short rawhide thongs with rocks at each end that Mexicans threw at the legs of cattle or deer to entwine them and bring them down.

"Might break the Ovaro's legs," Fargo fretted. "But I'd rather shoot him myself than know he's become an outlaw's horse. A plow horse has a better life than an owlhoot's mount."

Baylor unleashed his bolas with an expert fling that sent them spinning toward the Ovaro. The stallion's hind legs froze in midstride and he went crashing down hard, tumbling over and over and raising clouds of dust. When Dobie and Scooter Evans opened fire on the Tutt boy, Fargo raised holy hell with the Henry, levering and firing until his cheek was slapped numb.

Giving it up as a bad job, the pair of horse thieves fled into the hills. Fargo, worried the Ovaro was now permanently lamed, watched with baited breath while Baylor dismounted and knelt to loosen the bolas. Fargo gave a shrill whistle, and the stallion, shaken but still game, rose to his feet. Fargo felt like cheering when his pinto headed back toward him at a brisk trot, unharmed.

Mary Lou still stood beside Fargo in the rutted trail. Nonetheless, Baylor Tutt whipped out a .44 caliber Colt dragoon pistol as he rode up to join them, eyeing Fargo closely. He wore a flap hat with old burn marks where it had served as a pot holder.

"Vouch for him, sis?" Baylor asked. "Thissen ain't no farmer nor store clerk. 'Pears to me he's got the hard eyes of a hired killer."

"Can't vouch for him," Mary Lou replied while Fargo patted his Ovaro to calm him. "But this is Mr. Skye Fargo, and earlier today he kicked the crap outta Clay Evans in Lead Hill, then shot Hollis Maitland's gun clean from out his hand. Dobie and Scooter just tried to steal his horse. If he's a hired killer, big brother, he surely wasn't hired by Langston Evans and the Pukes."

"Well, don't it beat the Dutch!" Baylor swung down, a slight, wiry lad just into his twenties. He offered Fargo his hand. "Mister, word of that fight has spread like grease through a goose. Old Clay had an ace-high shit fit. You even buffaloed the sheriff after he already had the drop on you."

"Thanks," Fargo said. "But the neatest trick *I've* seen lately was you and those bolas. This is the best horse I've ever owned, Baylor, and you saved him. I'm much obliged."

Baylor, who saw few men of Fargo's appearance, had liked the tall stranger instantly.

"What was you two doing back there?" he asked his sister, meaning the secluded thicket behind her.

"Same thing you and Julianna Jones like to do back there," she retorted. Both of them laughed.

"We got a strict ma," Mary Lou explained to Fargo. "So me, Baylor, and my other brother, Jesse, we cover for each other."

Fargo had fallen silent, staring at the open, bloody wounds where the Ovaro had been lashed mercilessly.

"You just headed through?" Baylor asked. "Or do you plan on putting down roots?"

"I'll never sink down roots anyplace," he replied. "But the way I see it, I've been shot at, insulted, and had my horse stolen and badly used. It's personal now. I b'lieve I'll spread my blankets here for a few days and see if I can teach some old boys some manners."

4

"Ain't nobody knows for a fack this Devil's Mouth exists," Baylor explained during the short ride to the Tutt farm. "Old Langston Evans claimed his land under squatter's rights, but now he acts like one of the big bugs, and the courts back his claim. Now it's posted 'gainst trespassers, and his clan shoots anybody they catch on their land."

"But there's got to be a cave there on his land," Mary Lou insisted from behind Fargo. "A *big* one. You heard how the sound of all them horses just suddenly stopped."

"Missouri border is just spittin' distance from here," Baylor added. "All them Pukes can raid towns, rob banks, hold up trains and stagecoaches, then run down here and hide in Devil's Mouth. The Evanses don't just hide 'em, neither. They feed 'em and keep 'em supplied with horseflesh."

"Are they part of the Border Ruffians organization itself?"

Baylor snorted. "That's like trying to separate the water from the wet—it's all one."

"Clay Evans called me a Jayhawker abolitionist this morning," Fargo said. "So it's easy to believe he's at least sympathetic to the Border Ruffians."

Fargo added no more, but having been shot at by this Evans trash, then having his horse beaten and stolen by them, had made up his mind for him. Before he left Arkansas, the guilty parties would be either planted or jugged—preferably planted.

"Well, that's our place just yonder," Baylor said with evident pride as the trail emerged from woods to cleared land.

Fargo understood his pride. This was not just another half-section nester farm blighted by the local drought. It looked like at least a hundred-and-fifty acres, most of it under split-rail fences and irrigated from a broad stream.

"Not exactly a strip of side garden, huh?" Baylor asked.

"Not hardly," Fargo agreed, looking at the healthy sorghum and corn. "You folks are a credit to the land."

Fargo wasn't just being polite, he meant the praise. It took damn hard work to build this rustic homestead, and farmers fed the world. But in the process of turning dreams into deeds, much was being lost of the primitive wilderness it had been his pleasure to explore. The ax, rifle, boat, and horse were the tools that conquered the West. Now would come the plows, portable windmills, and steam shovels—the tools that would eventually erase the frontier.

They rode through a yard gate and several friendly hounds ran forward to sniff at the Ovaro. Fargo took in a typical frontier house of mud-chinked logs, only much larger than usual, with a slope-off kitchen extension at the back. Several shirttail towheads played in the yard.

"Somethin' you need to know," Mary Lou said low in Fargo's ear. "Pa was tossed from his horse a while back, hit his head hard on a rock. He's a mite . . . addled. But he's harmless. As for Ma . . . she's good people, Skye, but a hard life has turned her strict. She won't even tolerate

24

no laughing on the Lord's Day. The cholera plague back east took most of her people within a month. She never got over it."

Fargo nodded sympathetically. Mary Lou meant the 1840s epidemic that swept America and wiped out entire towns. It had been widely blamed on "godlessness."

They watered the horses from a rain barrel and left them to graze in lush grass behind the house, Fargo stripping his Ovaro down to the neck leather. He eyed the surrounding hills.

"The Evans bunch won't attack here," Baylor assured him. "It's a sorta unwrit treaty to pertect the wimmin and kids on both sides. We leave them in peace at home, they do the same for us. So far, anyhow."

"Anyplace else, though," Mary Lou said bitterly, "is open season. They killed our sister Dora and her husband on their way to church. Them's their kids in the yard, orphans now."

Her use of the word orphan made Fargo's jaw harden for a moment, as if some old memory chord had been plucked. However, his mood shifted quickly at his first glimpse of the interior of the Tutt home, which he found surprising and impressive.

Unlike most chinked-log houses, it did not contain the usual cowhide chairs and nail-keg stools. A big claw-footed dining table of solid hardwood was set with solid silver dinner plates. A bureau of carved oak filled a corner. Photographs were not yet common in this region, but evidently the entire Tutt family had been "sitting for the cutter" and had their silhouettes traced, cut, and mounted. These so-called poor man's photographs filled the wall above a fieldstone fireplace.

Fargo did a double take when he glanced into the parlor and saw a starling in a wooden cage. However, reminders of the feud were hard to miss—a peg on the nearest wall held a lead ladle for making bullets from a bar of pig lead.

Reigning over everything with patrician reserve was a silver-haired gent in a rocking chair. He wore a dress suit of black broadcloth and had prominent throat muscles like taut cords, his eyes sunken deep behind the cheekbones. A slightly younger woman occupied a cushioned chair beside him, darning socks.

"Pa," Mary Lou said, "I brung home company. This here's Mr. Skye Fargo."

Joshua Tutt leaned forward, eyes narrowing as he studied Fargo. "Nice lookin' fella, Mary Lou. You bunkin' with him?"

"Pa!" his daughter exclaimed. "Shame on you!"

"Nice lookin' fella," Pa Tutt insisted again. "He's sent his fair share of men to the farther side of Jordan, I'd wager. Catch a baby by him, it'll grow up a *man*, kill that Evans trash."

Ma Tutt was plagued by expensive false teeth that didn't fit. She slipped them out and set them in her lap. "I told you it's all them hot baths that girl takes, Pa. All that heat gets to workin' on her female regions. Leads to impure thoughts."

Despite his mother's stern visage, Baylor burst out laughing and Mary Lou slapped his arm. Fargo himself was hard-pressed to keep a straight face.

Ma Tutt gazed at Fargo. "Long as you ain't no snuff dipper, Mr. Fargo. I will not abide a snuff dipper."

Joshua Tutt waved his wife quiet and fixed Fargo with a profound stare. "Did you know, sir, a man dying of thirst can drink his own piss, and if he don't puke it out, he'll mebbe last another day? God's truth."

"Pa," Mary Lou scolded in a whisper, flushing to the roots of her hair.

In the ensuing silence, no one in the embarrassed family seemed to know where to look. Fargo did indeed know that fact, having been forced to do it while crossing New Mexico's Journey of Death. "Actually, Mr. Tutt, it's better if you can ice it."

Everyone laughed at Fargo's joke, including the old man. It was clear, however, that the patriarch of the Tutt clan was useless for commanding the defense of his family in a vicious feud. Fargo hoped, for the sake of the women and kids, that Baylor and his brother Jesse could handle the job or end the feud.

Everybody repaired to the summer kitchen for hot mince pie and coffee except for Pa Tutt, who took a glass of buttermilk to settle his stomach. A boy in a sack diaper, barely past infancy and his cheeks still plump with baby fat, sat in a corner spinning a top.

"That's little Billy," Mary Lou explained. "Our cousin Jenny's baby. Clay, Dobie, and Scooter Evans all three raped her afore they tossed her off Lookout Point."

"I'm awful sorry to hear it," Fargo said. "But there's been Evanses dying too, am I right?"

"Not women," she snapped, her face bewitching even in anger. "We've lost two on our side. A Tutt man," she added proudly, beaming at her brother, "takes his fight to the men."

Baylor scowled at the injustice of it. "They set it all in motion, Skye. For us, it's self-defense."

"Langston Evans is skunk-bit mean," Mary Lou insisted. "Skye, that man is so hateful he made all of his kids wear soaking-wet diapers just so's they'd grow up mean like him, which they done."

Fargo didn't poke any deeper, not when he was enjoying their hospitality. He was sure the Evans clan had their side of it, too, but frankly, if they were indeed rapists and woman killers as Mary Lou claimed, Fargo intended to bring down the thunder. He ignored most petty crimes, and even a few bigger ones, but he'd drop a bead on any man who harmed a woman.

As he tossed his plate into the wash bucket, he wondered about this rumored Devil's Mouth. The Evans clan had thrown down the gauntlet when they nabbed his horse and tried to ventilate Fargo. The Border Ruffians were the worst sort of lawless marauders, and proving the Evanses were aiding them would result in prison time for the Evanses under local sedition laws.

"This cave called Devil's Mouth," he said. "If large groups of riders can hide there, it must be big. How come no locals know where it is?"

"Them that's found it," Baylor replied, "don't live to report it. Langston Evans patrols his land like a soldier. My brother Jesse is looking for it right now."

"Starts a few miles up the road," Mary Lou said. "All hills and brushy hollows. Watch for the rail fences. But I'd fight shy of that place, Skye."

Old Joshua Tutt had been poring over Scripture while he drank his buttermilk. "Mr. Fargo," he called out, his face wrinkled in puzzlement. "You seem an intelligent man. I've dog-eared my Bible, and I'm clemmed if I can make head nor tail out of this: 'Joseph tied his ass to a tree and proceeded to Bethlehem.' Now, without his ass, a man's legs wouldn't be connected proper to his body, am I right?"

Mary Lou rolled those dark berry eyes at Fargo.

"Think I'll take a little squint around," he said, lifting his gun belt from a peg on the wall and buckling it on.

"Come back for supper," Mary Lou invited. "And, Skye? Be *mighty* careful. It's a darn shame, but law ain't never ruled around here. Just killers."

Fargo had already washed out the Ovaro's wounds and treated them with carbolic. With the stallion grazed and watered, Fargo bore due east toward the sprawling homestead of the Evans clan. The heated issue of Border Ruffians versus Jayhawkers didn't interest Fargo much—Arkansas was mostly a pro-slavery state, but not unanimously, and Fargo believed only criminals should be in chains. Still, his grudge at the moment was personal. He didn't like loud-mouthed louts like Clay and Dobie Evans, and Fargo meant to balance the ledger.

The late afternoon sun was hot and Fargo kept a wary eye out for ambushers as he held the Ovaro to a hard trot. He passed no one except a mail rider with a postbag tied to his saddle horn. Mail delivery out here was not exactly as regular as the equinox, and no great wonder. Not only did the great buffalo plains begin just west of Arkansas, so did the vast Indian Territory.

The road dipped, and Fargo saw about a dozen horses grazing in a draw behind a new split-rail fence. A distant, two-story house was painted a brilliant white.

"Not one of those horses comes from the same sire and dam," Fargo muttered, noticing the confusion of colors and markings: claybanks, sorrels, buckskins, blood bays, gingers. "Every damn one was likely stolen."

A nearly toothless rider on a mule approached Fargo. He touched his slouch hat. "Best not to take this road past the Evans place," he advised. "The old man uses passersby for target practice."

"Public road, innit?" Fargo asked.

"Not when the Big Boss decides otherwise. Most folks take the Pine Creek cutoff."

Fargo asked, "You work for him?"

"Yep, but I can't stomach the overbearing son of a buck. That's why I'm warning you."

Fargo's reply was cut short by a burst of gunfire from a wooded hilltop beyond the house. Loud shouts were followed by more gunshots. They weren't aimed at Fargo— not yet.

"Thanks for the warning!" Fargo shouted, thumping the Ovaro forward with his heels.

The Ovaro had plenty of stored bottom and welcomed the opportunity to stretch it out. The stranger's warning proved sound: as Fargo streaked past the Evans house, rifles opened up from several windows. One bullet flew so close it kissed his beard. Fargo shucked out his Colt, at a full gallop, and put out every window in the front of the house.

With the house receding behind him, Fargo turned his attention to the gun battle on the wooded hill. He circled around to the quiet side and, after riding to the crest of the hill, dismounted. By now bullets were whipping through the leaves everywhere. As a precaution, Fargo threw a headlock on the Ovaro and tugged him downward. The well-trained stallion had been taught to lie flat in heavy gunfire.

"Come and get it, you Puke sons of bitches!" a man's voice roared out, just ahead of Fargo. "I'll perforate your goddamn livers!"

It had to be Jesse Tutt. He was the spitting image of his brother, Baylor. Jesse's horse lay flat, too, but it wasn't from training—blood still plumed from a fatal shot to its neck. The young man had taken cover behind it.

Fargo yanked his Henry from its boot and started cautiously forward. "Don't shoot at me, Jesse!" he called out. "I'm joining the fight."

The youth whirled, but awkwardly—Fargo saw he was wounded just above the left elbow, his shirt saturated with blood.

"Yeah, sure, stranger," the kid retorted, thumb-cocking his long Kentucky rifle. "And pigs don't snort, neither."

"I'm a friend of your family, you dumb galoot. Your pa just got done explaining to me how a man can drink his own piss—that prove it?"

Despite the bullets hurtling in, Jesse's young face divided in a smile. "Good to see you, fella, these hounds been on me long enough. But it's best if you just skedaddle right now. I'm dead meat, and that's a hard-cash fact."

Fargo shook his head. "This is just another scrape. You'll be home before supper."

He took off his bandanna. "But tie off that wound first or you'll bleed out."

"All right, but bring that Henry closer and dose 'em with some Kentucky pills. I'm down to three shots."

Fargo low-crawled through the leaves and took cover behind the dead horse. He could see the attackers spread along the front slope, perhaps a dozen of them advancing on foot. Several wore the plumed hats of Missouri Border Ruffians. Bullets thumped into the dead horse.

"Load this," Fargo said, tossing Jesse his Colt and shell belt. "I ain't too sure we can turn 'em back quick. These boys are raised from birth to eat six-shooters."

Fargo had sixteen rounds in the Henry's tube magazine, but with this many attackers he couldn't afford to spray his rounds. Only when he had a sure target and a clean bead did he fire.

"Four shots, four Pukes popped over! That's holdin' and squeezin', mister," Jesse praised.

"The hell you doing up here?" Fargo asked during a lull in the fireworks. "A dozen to one ain't smart odds."

"They took me by surprise," the young hothead admitted. "That son of a bitch Langston Evans is hidin' a big cave on his land. The bastard ain't just sellin' boosted horses to the slaver gangs, he's hidin' the Pukes after they kill and plunder. I got the location narrowed down to this hill on account there's hoofprints all over. *Jee*-zus!"

Somebody below had just fired a big-bore gun that tore a fist-sized chunk out of the dead horse. All of a sudden, a blood-piercing warble went up from below.

"Shit!" Jesse went a few shades paler. Bullets thwapped in harder. "They're charging full bore, friend! I was you, I'd get on that fast horse a yourn and light a shuck outta here. It's me they want."

"Son, you got enough guts to fill a smokehouse. But you're too quick to dig your own grave. These ain't Texas Rangers charging us, just Missouri hardcases."

Fargo had learned to focus force at the enemy's strongest point of attack, knowing the weaker flanks would fold once the main body was stopped.

"I just reloaded, so I've got sixteen shots, you got six," he told Jesse. "This time don't bother to aim—spread your shots between that heart-shaped boulder and that lightning-split tree. *Now*, boy!"

One of the Border Ruffians had recklessly decided to lead the charge from horseback. Fargo squatted on his heels, drew a bead, and wiped the man from the saddle. A hammering racket of gunfire exploded through the hills, and human cries punctuated the gunplay as man after man dropped, dead or wounded. Fargo had called it right—the sheer number of unexpected casualties sent the rest back to their horses and fleeing, whipping up their mounts until yellow-brown dust choked the trail.

Fargo properly introduced himself and took a few minutes for a better look at Jesse's wound.

"Your clover was deep this time. The bullet was small caliber and passed right through," Fargo said. "I'll wash it with carbolic so it won't mortify. Prob'ly won't even leave a scar."

"Long way from my heart," Jesse dismissed it. "I'm already carrying two slugs in my hide, and brother Baylor's got three."

"No offense," Fargo said as he retied the wound again. "But these damn feuds help nobody but the undertaker. We need to leave 'em back east in the hill country, not export 'em out west where there's already plenty of violence."

"Just 'cause two clans get to fighting," Jesse reminded him, "don't mean they're *both* criminal trash. Or that both get equal shares in the blame. Our people, sure, we sell moonshine, but mostly we farm and raise hogs. But that Evans trash, they're organized horse thieves and tight as ticks with the Pukes. Murderers, too, the whole bunch."

Fargo nodded as he helped Jesse onto the Ovaro. "Yeah, I had a little set-to with Clay Evans this morning. Then, a little later, with his brother Dobie and cousin Scooter. I have to agree—*none* of those human buzzards will win jewels in paradise."

"You look like a good man, Mr. Fargo," Jesse said.

"And you just proved how fightin' scrapes is old hat to you. But you've stumbled into a snake den now. Best to dust your hocks outta here."

Actually, Fargo agreed. Pure instinct always pointed him west—it was the empty spaces that rejuvenated a man, not these damned settlements. However, there came a point where it was better to stand pat.

"Well, the attempt to shoot me—that I could overlook," Fargo agreed. "Ain't like it's rare. Hell, sometimes I think there's a big red target painted on my ass. But I got a sorta soft spot for my stallion. We've trailed together for years, and he's saved my bacon dozens of times. So when some pond scum not only tries to steal him, but lays him open with a whip, there's a reckoning coming. I mean to stay on those Evans boys like heat rash."

"Can't say that breaks my heart," Jesse said behind him. "You may not choose to fight alongside us Tutts, not the way you talk and look—you're a lone maverick, I'd wager. But it's good to know you're in the fight."

"In it to win it," Fargo assured him, "after I find out a little more about this Evans bunch. I ain't one to put the noose before the gavel."

"Finding out about that bunch won't take long. Just slap that jackleg 'sheriff' around a little—Hollis Maitland will squeal like a hog under the blade."

Fargo squelched his own reply, suddenly aware of how the Ovaro's ears had pricked forward. The trail, at this point, was narrow and closely grown on both sides with thick brush.

"Fill your hand," Fargo said tensely to Jesse. "Watch the right side of the trail. I'll take the left. They've left a dry-gulcher behind."

For perhaps another thirty seconds they rode, hearing the mournful whisper of wind in the trees, the pulsating hum of insects.

"Nah, they'll be busy doubling back around to their cave," Jesse decided, letting his hammer down. "We're all right—*God Almighty*!"

The split-second attack was ingenious. With a vicious, full-throated snarl, a huge yellow cur leaped out of the bushes and sank its teeth into the Ovaro's left foreleg. This was intended to make the stallion rear in panic, but the trail-hardened Ovaro stood steady.

"Watch out!" Jesse screamed when two shotgun barrels, sawed off to about ten inches, poked out of the bushes near Fargo. At the same time Fargo glimpsed a vacant-eyed, rabbit-toothed man who, except for a wild shock of red hair, showed the Evans line in his features.

"Scooter Evans, you mother-ruttin' coward!" Jesse roared out.

There wasn't even a full second for Fargo to make the call. The man himself was hidden now, leaving no target. Yet that scattergun was about to blow them to rag tatters. Counting on his aim, Fargo picked the left shotgun barrel and fired his Colt, sending the slug rocketing right down the barrel.

With an ear-shattering explosion, Fargo's perfectly aimed slug detonated the shotgun shell in its chamber, shattering the breach of the gun. Scooter Evans screamed like a soul in torment, and when he jumped into view Fargo saw his face was a mass of bleeding pits. He fled into the brush, still howling, as he tossed shots over his shoulder with a sidearm.

The vicious cur was showing no mercy, and Fargo broke its spine with his next shot. When Jesse started to leap down, planning to chase Scooter, Fargo restrained him with a hand to the shoulder. "It's sucker bait," the Trailsman warned him. "They'll have more waiting. Same way Indians kill the cavalry, by goading them into a chase."

Jesse nodded, seeing the logic of it. "Mr. Fargo, that was some shootin'. Talk about threadin' a needle."

"Actually, I got lucky," Fargo admitted. "But luck ain't the boy to count on. Jesse, you folks got a rat's nest in the hills, and it's got to be cleaned out quick—damn quick. Otherwise the rats will overrun the entire state of Arkansas and kill everything decent."

5

Langston Evans, wrapped in a Prince Albert frock coat, paced up and down the length of his home's double parlor, apoplectic with rage. He was called the Big Boss because his leonine head and impressive silver mane of hair reminded many of the other Big Boss, out in Utah Territory, Brigham Young. Evans had been forced to leave his native Kentucky after being indicted for illegal dealings with Indians, to whom he had sold whiskey and weapons.

"I nary once seen such female, chicken-gutted foolishness!" he fumed. "*Two* men routing a dozen enemies that are coming at 'em like the devil beating bark. And just why was that little cock chafer Jesse Tutt pokin' around on our hill? Bullfrog hunting?"

A sofa and several wing chairs were occupied by sullen, shamefaced men: Clay and Dobie Evans, their cousin Scooter, and James "Jimbo" Powers, leader of a Border Ruffians gang active along the Arkansas-Missouri border. Matilda "Maw-maw" Evans sat in a rocking chair, braiding rags for a rug. She was present at every meeting, and reputedly meaner than a badger in a barrel. Many said she was the true leader of the Evans faction.

"Hell, Pa," Clay replied, "with all the men and horses using the cave, its location was bound to get discovered. But the escape tunnel is still safe."

"Ballocks! If they can find the cave, they can find the tunnel. We did."

"But, Pa, nobody has even found the cave yet," Dobie, the youngest boy, pointed out. "That's a mighty big hill, and the entrance is hid real good."

Langston turned red to his earlobes. "Shut pan, whelp, afore I brain ye!"

"Sorry, Pa," Dobie muttered.

"*Sorry?* Politeness, in a man, is a sign of weakness," his mother snapped. "I'll hear no more apologies from you or you'll wear a shawl."

"Nobody can find the cave, eh?" old man Evans repeated, his tone mocking the words. "Both you boys are the hog-stupid shame of my loins. I talked to that worthless Hollis Maitland, and I've kallated the facts—that bearded bastard helping the Tutts is named Skye Fargo. Sometimes known as the Trailsman."

Neither of the Evans boys or their cousin reacted to the news, for they read very little and had not traveled widely. Jimbo Powers, however, loosed a string of curses.

"That explains it," he said, nodding his balding head. "How he turned us back, I mean. Only a man of Fargo's mettle could pull that off."

"So what is your remedy?" Langston demanded. "Just get snow in your boots and run? Right when we've got a bullion coach headed our way, loaded with new-minted gold coins?"

"Hell, no. It was Fargo's choice to fight agin us. Now he's been warned to roll his blankets and clear out. If he don't, we kill him. I got two dozen men and can add more. And there's four more between you Evanses. He can't know this area as good as we do."

"Just remember," Maw-maw Evans put in, rocking once again, "the best time to kill a man is when he's thigh deep in water or taking a crap. This is *our* territory, we know every holler and tree. Just keep him in sight and the opportunity *will* crop up. I guarantee it. Every man must crap— I killed a landlord thataway."

"The timing could not be worse," Langston fretted, still pacing. "Old Joshua Tutt was a reg'lar hellhound till that horse skull-kicked him and turned him loco. With him useless, his kin had turned all holler and no heart. Now this goddamn Skye Fargo turns up to rally 'em."

"Scooter," Maw-maw said, "I see your uncle Langston is gettin' worked up to a fare-thee-well. I can also see that vein a-throbbin' on his temple. Pour him some antifogmatic. Pour yourself one, too. That face must hurt powerful bad."

Pony glasses and a decanter of potent whiskey sat on the

fireplace mantel. Scooter filled two glasses and gave one to his uncle, who tossed it back like sugar water.

"Boys, we're gonna go the whole hog," the patriarch announced. "There ain't no damn 'feud.' The whole business is spoze to've commenced when I kilt Sam Tutt in revenge for murdering my bother Daniel. But Daniel was a birdbrain and kilt hisself cleaning his rifle. Them Tutts are sittin' on the best bottomland in this hull damn state. If we just murder 'em, the law dogs will come after us. But a *feud*—now that's where the law steps wide."

Evans had ample reasons for his confidence. The regional violence was coming from every level of government, too, including state-sanctioned murder. It began two decades earlier when Missouri governor Lillburn Boggs issued his Extermination Order against Mormons.

"But, Pa," Clay put in, "once we kill 'em all off, that land ain't worth a whorehouse token withouten a legal deed."

"That'll be left to Judge Moneybags, son. He ain't failed me yet."

"Once you get that land," Jimbo Powers said, "you get you some African darkies to pick the cotton and you'll be one of the cotton kings. Got me a brother in east Texas, he cleared thirty thousand dollars on this year's crop."

"You'll be rolling in it, too," Langston reminded the Border Ruffian, "once you knock off that bullion coach. Just remember—my spies got the information it was coming, and I'm lettin' you and your boys keep all the swag. But that means you keep on helping me for a spell—especially with Skye Fargo now in the mix."

"A man of Fargo's caliber has to be respected," Powers replied. "But he puts his pants on one leg at a time, just like every other man. My boys are rough-and-tumble Missouri stock, veterans of Indian wars, the Mexican War, prisons. . . . Hell, they're always on the scrap, and they'll go after Fargo like dogs to raw meat."

Scooter gingerly touched his ravaged face. "Fargo's in rut for Mary Lou Tutt and goes to their place. To hell with this truce about not attacking each other's house. Why'n't we just wait till Fargo's there, then unleash Jimbo's boys?"

Langston stopped pacing and weighed the suggestion for a full minute. "I said we're goin' the whole hog, and I meant it. They say it's wise to be shifty in a new country—that's how you get set up for respectability. We'll make another try or two to snuff Fargo without waking snakes. If that don't work, we'll catch him at the Tutt place and shoot the hull bunch of 'em to doll stuffing."

Before Fargo did anything else, after the ambush attempt on him and Jesse Tutt had been foiled, he dug out his bottle of carbolic acid and carefully washed out the dog bites on the Ovaro's foreleg. That cur had behaved as if distempered, and Arkansas was noted for its packs of savage wild dogs, often rabid. Was it just coincidence that Scooter and the dog seemed to function as a team?

"I don't know," Fargo worried aloud when he finished. "A couple of those punctures look deep. I hate to do it, but I'd best cauterize the wounds."

With Jesse keeping a close eye on the trail in both directions, Fargo built a sparse mound of kindling and small sticks. He removed a piece of oilskin from his possibles bag, opening it to reveal a handful of lucifers. He thumb-scratched one of the matches to life, grateful he wasn't forced to use his flint and steel—some progress Fargo embraced.

"Don't stand behind him like that, Jesse," Fargo warned. "Once the blade hits that wound, he *will* kick."

Quick was best, and Fargo wasted no time. The moment the blade of the Arkansas toothpick glowed red-orange, he pivoted toward the Ovaro and laid it over the bites. A sizzle of cooking meat, an ear-shattering whicker, and the stallion not only mule-kicked, he went straight up and chinned the moon.

Fargo immediately splashed cool water on the cauterized area, and the stalwart pinto, much like his master often did, took the pain in silence.

"That hoss is right off the top shelf," Jesse praised. "I just had a damn good one killed by that Puke bunch. Mr. Fargo, keep a close eye on your stallion—that Evans trash are hoss-stealin' sons of bitches."

Fargo gave a rueful nod. "I learned the hard way. Your brother Baylor saved my horse earlier today."

Jesse grinned. "Bet he used them Mexer doodads, huh?"

"*Bolas*, yeah. That jasper is mighty good with 'em."

"I'll tell the world he's good. He can drop anything from a charging bull to a runaway horse."

By now the Ovaro, though still snorting in discomfort, was able to place weight on his wounded leg.

"It's a short distance to your place now," Fargo said, glancing at the westering sun. "Mind if we lead my horse? Two riders might tax that leg."

"Mr. Fargo, I'll *carry* that hoss if you'druther. Thanks to both of you, I'm still above the ground."

"We *are* magnificent sons of bitches," Fargo agreed, and both men laughed.

With Fargo holding the bridle reins in one hand, his Henry in the other, the two men and the Ovaro had an uneventful hike to the Tutt place, not counting a brief run-in with a pair of porcupines—except that, even here in Arkansas, the West transformed everything into its image: Jesse called them by their mountain-man name, "prickly beavers."

"I reckon you been jist about ever'place, huh?" Jesse asked. "You don't appear to be the kind who roosts in one spot too long."

"I'm a westering wanderer," Fargo admitted, "though I've been east of the Great Waters plenty."

He used the Indian name for the Mississippi River.

"You seen big cities, too?"

"Oh, been to Chicago and New Orleans, a few others."

Jesse whistled. "Ain't that the beatingest? Biggest town I seed is Memphis."

Fargo could have included many other big cities he had visited all over the country, but their soulless roar had always sent him packing. Outside of women, whiskey, and good eats, most cities held no lure for him.

"You must be hungry," Jesse said. "Ma'll cowhide me if I don't talk you into takin' vittles with us. Ma, she's a mite Bible-thumpin' at times, but that woman sets the best table in Arkansas."

"I'm so hungry I damn near shot that skunk back on the trail," Fargo admitted.

As the Tutt spread loomed into view, however, Fargo faced a thorny problem: exactly where to leave the Ovaro. The Tutts, like many farmers, simply left their horses in a grassy meadow behind the house. None of their animals, however, compared to the Ovaro in the eyes of a horse thief. Also, the Tutt animals would all carry the usual brand on their left hips, whereas Fargo never branded a horse.

Jesse seemed to read Fargo's thoughts. "See that little copse of dogwood trees just past the house? You could tether your stallion there. It's got a little rill that ain't dried up yet like every other damn thing around here."

"That'll do," Fargo agreed, taking a careful glance around. "Just so long as we ain't being observed."

"Can't guarantee that," Jesse admitted. "Plenty of spies lately."

Fargo laughed when he spotted a sign he'd missed earlier, nailed to a tree: ALL GRASSHOPPERS KEEP OFF!!!

"Your spread looks fine," he praised. "You folks were smart to dig irrigation canals. This being rich bottomland don't hurt, either."

"God's truth. But I'm thinkin' that's why them Evans trash are tryin' to murder us Tutts off—so's they can take our land. Ain't just the Evans clan, neither—there's plenty of honest folks hurtin' bad on account a this drought. All these crooked-as-catshit 'rainmakers' are costin' folks their entire savings."

By now Fargo had put the Ovaro on a long tether, well hidden in the dogwood copse. He stripped the stallion down to the neck lather and spread the sweat-soaked saddle blanket out to dry.

"You know," Fargo remarked as both men hoofed it to the house, "usually, common troubles like drought will knit neighbors. Now, supposedly, there's a feud going on. All right, but I notice how one side—the Evans faction—not only keep trying to kill me, but to steal my horse. They also own a phony sheriff who spits when they saw hawk. The Tutts, on the other hand, have tossed no lead my way and even feed me. Jesse, you're right. This 'feud' business, however it got started, is just a smoke screen for a criminal landgrab."

Jesse gave an eager nod. "That's what I tell Pa, too, though he ain't so brain clear nowadays. What I can't figure is why, all of a sudden, seems zif they're in a big damn hurry to get the dirty business over. Before, they took their own sweet time."

"Might be a good answer," Fargo replied. "There's been talk back east for years about a new Homestead Act that'll grant dirt-cheap parcels of land—first come, best served. Rumors are thick that it's close to passage. Once it is, some already existing claims will be recognized, others declared illegal."

Jesse let out a whistle. "Well, bless my buttons! If that law passes, everybody out west can get set for a flood of land-grabbers and false deeds—not to mention fresh killings."

Fargo nodded. "Right now, most of you farmers are officially squatters. Those, like your family, who have proved up the land with homes and whatnot, will be granted clear title. I'd bet my horse the Evanses are hoping to be tenants here when the Homestead Act passes, if it ever does."

Jesse's clean-shaven face went crimson with rage. "They mean to wipe out our entire line and steal everything we've busted our humps to build."

" 'Fraid so," Fargo said as they reached the yard and several friendly hounds sniffed his buckskins curiously. "I'm all for honest law and order. But these damned Philadelphia lawyers in government are real good at passing these sweeping new laws, then failing to oversee them."

Baylor Tutt, sweating from fieldwork, met them in the yard and went into the house with them. The day was hot and humid, but a lively cross breeze from plenty of sash windows kept the house cool. Mary Lou, her shiny russet hair pulled back into a braided coil on her nape, pulled Fargo aside as he was unbuckling his gun belt in the entrance hall.

"Howdy, Mr. Buckskins," she greeted him with a coy up-and-under look. "What we done earlier, down near the stream? I liked it *just* fine. But we only got to the trimmings, not the main course. We got unfinished business."

A toothy grin flashed through Fargo's beard. He hung his gun belt from a peg and leaned his Henry against the wall.

"Music to my ears," he assured her, taking in those blackberry eyes and flawless skin, smooth as lotion. "Got your own bedroom? I'm good with windows."

She slugged his arm. "I'll just bet you are. Prob'ly been butt shot a few times, too, goin' *out* them windows, you hunka man heat."

Mary Lou lowered her voice so her brothers couldn't hear. "I do have my own bedroom, Skye, but we dursn't meet there. See, I'm a mite . . . loud when I'm bein' pleasured right. 'Sides, Ma found a pisser in my room once and, laws, she had a conniption fit."

Mary Lou meant a pessary, a device sold "for collapsed wombs" but actually used by women to prevent pregnancy.

Voices were suddenly raised within the house, and Fargo and Mary Lou joined the rest of the family. Ma Tutt was examining Jesse's wounded arm, her face an iron mask of sternness.

"Boy, are you tellin' me you rode onto Evans land all by your lonesome? After they kilt *two* of your close kin and left their youngens orphans? I guess you figure *you're* the biggest toad in the puddle now your pa's been hurt. Well, not by a jugful! Baylor is still your big brother, and Pa is *still* the man of this house."

Jesse, who obviously respected his mother, stood wretchedly mute, offering neither confirmation nor denial. Evidently, the memory of her murdered kin cost her a pang. Ma Tutt wiped her work-hardened hands on her muslin apron, a tear springing from one eye. She hugged her youngest son. "Well, you're alive, son, and for that I thank the good Lord."

"Yes, ma'am, and thanks to Mr. Fargo, too. He shooed them Pukes off like varmints from a chicken coop."

Just then, however, old Joshua Tutt wandered into the double parlor, buttoning his suspender loops to his pants—evidently emerging from a necessary trip out back. His rheumy eyes studied Fargo with friendly confusion. "Mr. Fargold, is it?"

"Fargo, sir," the Trailsman corrected him. "Skye Fargo."

"Fine name for a well-knit man. Mary Lou, get hitched to *this* one and he'll sire a fine line of Evans killers."

"Hesh, Pa," Mrs. Tutt scolded gently. "Mr. Fargo ain't here to get married, he's having supper with us."

"The truth cries out in the streets," Pa Tutt retorted, "yet no man ever heeds it."

"Hesh, Pa," Ma Tutt said again. "You're spoutin' gibberish. Wash up for supper."

"Gibberish, my sweet aunt! The Bard of Avon wrote that. And here's one that caps the climax."

Fargo watched Tutt pull a copy of the popular *Leslie's Weekly* from under one arm.

" 'Nothing of importance happened today,' " the old man read. "Know who writ that line in his diary? King George the Third of England—on July 4, 1776!"

Fargo grinned, appreciating the irony. "I reckon news traveled a mite slow in them powdered-wig days."

A bunch of children, several still toddlers, had followed the men into the house, curious about the tall stranger in dusty buckskins. Orphaned by the feud, Fargo recalled, his heart going out to them. He had taken a sack of sassafras candy from a saddlebag and now gave each of them a piece.

"Skye Fargo, that beard of yours is a sin to Crockett!" Mary Lou exclaimed, pulling a twig out of it. "Afore you push your legs under the dinner table, let me comb it out. Ma's partic'lar about beards."

"Long as he ain't no snuff dipper," Ma called out from the slope-off kitchen, where she was cooking dinner. Fargo noticed her cooking fuel was corncobs soaking in a bucket of coal oil.

Fargo dutifully plopped down in a ladder-back chair while Mary Lou went to work on his beard with a horn comb. He suspected this was all a ruse so she could tantalize him by pressing her firm breasts into him while she worked. Her lilac perfume didn't hurt any, either.

"Did you like what I done to you earlier today?" she whispered, combing bits of grass and leaves from his beard.

"Liked it just fine, dumplin'. Like you said, though—we got business to finish. Earlier today, that was just priming the pump."

For a moment she slipped one hand inside his shirt, playing with the curlicues of chest hair. "Boy, I'm gonna have you howlin' at the moon. I been slippery all day just thinkin' 'bout that war club inside me."

Just then Fargo thought he heard a distant whicker that sounded like the Ovaro, but with Mary Lou getting him all distracted he lost the thought before it could sink in.

"Soup's on!" Ma Tutt called from the dining room.

The smaller children had their own table in a corner. Fargo sat at the long oak table with Mary Lou, Baylor, Jesse, Joshua, and Ma Tutt. Fargo, starved for hot, home-cooked food, felt his mouth watering when Ma laid out a feast of corn pone and back ribs plus bean soup with dumplings.

Fargo picked up his knife to begin, but Joshua bowed his head and everyone else followed suit.

"We thank the Father, the Son, and the Holy Ghost; he who eats the fastest gets the most. Amen."

"Pa!" Ma scolded, slipping her false teeth in so she could eat. "Blasphemy right in front of Mr. Fargo! Shame on you."

"I think Skye forgives Pa," Mary Lou said sarcastically, for Fargo's mouth was already full.

"Mebbe Mr. Fargo ain't no Bible-raised man," Jesse said, "but thunderation! Y'all shoulda seed him rescue me when them Pukes was headed toward Devil's Mouth. He was a reg'lar tiger in a whirlwind."

" 'Less you *find* this Devil's Mouth, little brother," Baylor reminded him, "it don't exist. You keep your ass off that Evans property, hear? I can still whup you, boy."

"And if you try to run from your whipping, Jessie," Fargo cracked, "Baylor will drop you with his bolas."

Jesse took all this ribbing with a good-natured grin. "Ahh . . . *damn*, Baylor, you oughter seen what Mr. Fargo done to Scooter Evans' ugly face. Blowed his shotgun up with a bullet aimed right down a barrel. Scooter looked like a flock a crows worked his face over."

"That's a tonic," Baylor agreed, laughing outright. A moment later, however, he added, "Best take a care, Mr. Fargo. That pack of curs live for hard revenge agin their enemies. All them Evanses're trouble, and Clay and Scooter the worst of the pack. Scooter stabbed a bank clerk to death, in Lead Hill, just for givin' him Eastern money 'steada gold."

"Let me guess," Fargo said, taking a drink of cool applejack. "Sheriff Hollis Maitland ruled it self-defense?"

This coaxed a laugh from all the adults, even brain-addled Joshua Tutt.

"Sheriff, you say? My friend, Hollis ain't nothin' but a bootlicker for the Evans clan," Baylor said.

"Yeah, I figured that out right off," Fargo said. "But it's funny—he didn't strike me as the type who's naturally bent."

Jesse nodded, swallowing. "You can read men pretty

good, Mr. Fargo. Hollis is scared, not crooked. He's got a wife and a younger sister with two pups on the rug. Happens the Evans bunch do for him, Hollis' kin will starve."

It was a familiar pattern to the well-traveled Trailsman—using fear, violence, and bribes to control the woefully undermanned law officers. One shot in a dark alley could end an honest lawman's career.

Just then one of the coal-oil lamps on the table guttered out. Old Joshua opened his shirt and used a pocketknife to cut a new wick from his long-handles. He was relighting the lamp when Fargo again heard a whicker—definitely the Ovaro's.

He scraped back from the table, swiping at his mouth with a napkin. "Folks, if you'll excuse me—I need to check on my horse."

When Baylor and Jesse started to rise, Fargo waved them back down. " 'Preciate it, fellows, but one man is harder to spot than three."

Fargo grabbed his Henry and slipped out a side window into the grainy darkness of twilight. Hugging the cover of the log house, he levered a round into the Henry's chamber. Then he headed toward the nearby copse where he'd left the Ovaro.

6

By long habit from scouting amidst hostiles, Fargo moved cat-footed, avoiding the open lane. He was puzzled by the conflicting evidence. On the one hand, the Ovaro had definitely signaled trouble; on the other, all was quiet now. Perhaps, after all, it was simply a foraging raccoon or possum that startled the stallion.

However, Fargo always assumed there was trouble until he'd proved otherwise. He crept closer to the little copse of trees, eyes and ears alert. Night heat could be even more suffocating than day heat, and sweat beaded under the brim of his hat.

"That's it, boy, just stand easy," said a soft voice from inside the copse. "Cranky Man ain't here tó hurt you."

The English was good, spoken with a slight accent Fargo couldn't quite place. Another piece to the puzzle fell into place when he spotted an Indian pony hobbled beside the lane. The dish-faced skewbald wore a flat, stuffed buffalo-hide saddle.

"Easy, big fella, easy," the voice soothed. "Cranky Man just wants big medicine, anh? Rest easy."

Walking on his heels, Fargo entered the copse, the Henry's muzzle preceding him. There was light enough to reveal a heavyset, half-blood Choctaw Indian kneeling on the ground. Fargo could make out his beaded moccasins, fringed leggings, and deerskin shirt. He had left his saddle near the Ovaro, and now the Choctaw was pawing through the saddlebags. Despite the Indian's good English, he obviously clung to some tribal beliefs—he wore brightly colored magic pebbles on a string around his neck.

"What bit you, boy?" the intruder asked, spotting the fresh wound on the Ovaro's foreleg. "Good patch job, though. You'll be fine."

Normally, Fargo would have challenged an intruder by now. Most often, when he caught Indians searching his gear, they were looking for the black medicine—coffee. This Choctaw, however, had him immensely curious—the Ovaro was no horse to tolerate strangers. Yet he was calmly taking off the grass as if nothing unusual was happening. This Indian had extraordinary ability with horses. Besides—why hang around when he could simply steal everything and tote up his booty later?

Fargo's curiosity turned to outright amusement as the Choctaw seemed to ignore everything of value in the saddlebags, including brass-framed field glasses most Indians would value greatly as big magic. He did eat one strip of buffalo jerky, but left the rest of Fargo's trail rations untouched.

"*Here's* medicine," the Choctaw suddenly exclaimed, loosing a sigh of great contentment.

At first Fargo was utterly confused when the Choctaw

reverently pulled an old, empty envelope from the bottom of the bag. It had contained nothing but a routine pay voucher from the War Department, and Fargo had picked it up months ago at Fort Gibson in the Indian Territory.

However, as the strange intruder studied the envelope in the dying light, as if it were a holy prayer plume, Fargo realized why, his lips spreading in a grin. Many Indians greatly valued discarded envelopes, believing there was strange, potent magic in white man's calligraphy.

"Brash as a government mule, ain't you?" Fargo asked as he stepped into view. "I take it you must be Cranky Man?"

The half-blood Choctaw rose slowly to his feet, knee-caps popping.

"I'm a Digger Indian," Cranky Man said, thumping his chest. "Proud Digger."

Fargo caught the sarcasm. "Digger Indians" was not the name of a single real tribe, but meant any tribe that had been squeezed out of its homeland and forced into a primitive existence.

"So who butters your bread, mister?" Cranky Man asked, his voice belligerent. "The Jayhawkers or the Border Ruffians?"

"I see how you got your name. And you're a bold son of a bitch, are'ncha? All set to boost my horse, eat my grub, read my mail, and you ask *me* which criminal gang I ride with?"

"I can't read," Cranky Man said, "and I never stole a horse in my life, though I've pinched a few cows. Friend, knowing what your people do to *whites* who steal horses, you think a red son like me would try it? Far as that jerky I ate—did the buffalo give it to you?"

Fargo laughed. "Hell, I don't care about the grub, eat what you need. You're also welcome to that useless envelope. I don't think you meant to take my horse, either—you've got your own horse out in the lane."

"Horse, my ass! It's a tub of glue."

Fargo lowered the Henry. "My name's Fargo. Skye Fargo."

"Fargo . . . not the man some call the Trailsman?"

"I'm afraid that would be me, yeah."

"Damn my eyes, Mr. Fargo. Every tribe in the Nations talks about you, and most of the talk is good."

"Thanks. But speaking of the Nations . . . what are you doing in Arkansas?"

"Not a damn thing, been bone idle all my life," Cranky Man bragged. "Never met a true red man yet who could stomach hard labor. Actually I'm only a half-breed—my old man was a white soldier."

Fargo shook his head, realizing the Choctaw was being deliberately evasive. All five Civilized Tribes—Choctaws, Chickasaws, Cherokees, Creeks, and Seminoles—had been forced out of their ancient homeland, the Southeast, into the vast Indian Territory just west of Arkansas. Naturally they stayed as far east as they could, on the reservation, to be closer to the Southern climate and terrain they were used to. Some inevitably jumped the rez completely to enter Kansas or Arkansas and haze off white man's beef.

"Cranky Man," Fargo said bluntly, "*all* human life is cheap right now in this region. You get caught by Pukes or Jayhawkers, they'll have your head on a pole. I believe every man has a right to roam free, but the U.S. Army ain't open-minded."

An 1830 treaty had granted the Choctaw nation "a tract of land west of the Mississippi" as compensation for their expropriated homeland. That "tract," however, kept shrinking and shifting.

"Fair or not, it's safer for you to ride back home," Fargo added.

"Home?" Cranky Man loosed a bark of laughter. "I'm still looking for it."

"In *my* saddlebag?"

What happened next was so fast, so efficient, and so unexpected that even the famous Trailsman was caught flat-footed. Cranky Man instantly tripped him, toppling him to the leafy ground. Fargo had not noticed a weapon on the Choctaw, but his right hand flew to a sheath worn under his collar in back, emerging with a bone-handle knife with a blade of shiny black obsidian.

Fargo's Henry went flying when he was tripped. Worse, he landed on his holster side, trapping his Colt. He rolled desperately to draw it even as Cranky Man's arm flew back to throw the lethally honed knife.

Fargo, you double-barreled greenhorn, the Trailsman chastised himself, *looks like it's curtains now.*

He managed to clear leather and thumb-cock his Colt. However, Cranky Man wasn't even looking at him when he threw. The knife streaked from his hand, a rifle spoke its deadly piece behind Fargo, and Cranky Man's greasy flap hat whirled off his head like a child's spinning top. There was a harsh grunt of pain, brief choking noises, then a crashing of bushes as someone toppled.

"Don't shoot me, white-skin!" Cranky Man shouted at Fargo, whose hand was still filled with blue steel. "That bullet just now was meant for your back."

"*Shoot* you, you ugly red son?" Fargo said, climbing to his feet. "I might just kiss you."

"I'd prefer being shot, hair-face."

Cranky Man's knife had buried itself to the haft in the ambusher's bony chest. Fargo saw, from a glance at his plumed hat and butternut-dyed clothing, he was a Border Ruffian, almost surely one of Jim Powers' faction.

"Dirty damn Pukes," Cranky Man spat out. "They kill the red man and keep the black man in chains."

"As you *might* have noticed just now," Fargo reminded him, dusting off his trousers, "they kill plenty of whites, too."

"Yeah, they do," Cranky Man conceded. "So they ain't all bad. But if they want your hide, Fargo, you must be a good man. Friends?"

"Honored," Fargo assured him, and the two men shook hands. "That was one of the quickest knife kills I've seen."

"Do I still have to ride home?" Cranky Man asked slyly.

Fargo laughed. "Old son, I'm no longer worried about you taking care of yourself—or me. I do hope your . . . activities are mostly legal."

"That word 'mostly,'" Cranky Man said, "should be chewed a little finer."

Fargo laughed. "Where you staying?"

"An old cave in the river bluffs between Lead Hill and Diamond City. Ain't but a twenty-minute ride from here. Plenty of room for two and there's plenty of graze for the horses. One problem—you can almost piss across the Missouri border from there. Pukes are thicker than ticks on a hog."

"Skye? Skye, Christ, you all right? Sing out, boy, or we come in a-smokin'!"

It was Jesse Tutt's worried voice.

"All clear, boys, thanks to this flea-bit blanket ass who fights like a demon unleashed. C'mon in."

"Moses on the mountain!" Baylor exclaimed when the fading light disclosed the dead Border Ruffian.

"You fellows can have his horse," Cranky Man said after a quick look at the outlaw's nearby ginger gelding. "Ain't worth an old underwear button to me. Been rode hard and put away wet too many times, and its feet are bad. Should be a good trottin'-to-town horse, though. You can have that hogleg pistol, too—it's cap and ball, too much work for me. Think I'll keep this New Haven Arms repeating rifle, though. Trophy of war."

Cranky Man yanked his knife out of the corpse and wiped the blade clean along the dead man's trousers. Baylor and Jesse watched the Choctaw from wary eyes.

Cranky Man laughed gruffly. "You both got a fine head of hair, boys, but don't fret. Some Choctaws do scalp, but me, I'm like the Apaches out west—I puke when I try it."

"Now, look-a-here, that's mighty tall talk," Baylor protested, but Fargo pushed both their rifle barrels down.

"Boys, this is Cranky Man," he explained. "Drop your muzzles. He hates Pukes the way horses hate bears. And he just saved my bacon when this murdering slug tried to backshoot me. Cranky Man, meet Baylor and Jesse Tutt."

"Say," Baylor said, "ain't you a pretty good horse peeler, Cranky Man? Broke some horses to leather for the Evans clan last summer?"

"I done that, yeah, but only until I finally figured out the horses were stolen from wild herds captured in Texas."

"Boys, this neighborly little confab is over," Fargo announced. "Someone will be coming soon to check out the rifle shot. Don't forget, not only is the main bunch of Pukes camped just north of here in Missouri, but we got our own nest holed up even closer on Evans land. Or so Jesse claims, and I've seen evidence he's right."

"Devil's Mouth, yessir," Jesse insisted in his hillman's twang. "Roomy cave with an escape tunnel. This hull damn territory is crawlin' with kill-crazy sons of bucks who got nothin' to lose and will shoot a man for his boots."

"That's why you and your brother need to hightail it back to the house," Fargo advised, tossing the saddle onto

49

the Ovaro and cinching the girth. "I don't want this killing blamed on you Tutts, or the truce about not attacking each other's houses might crumble. So I'm gonna dump the body a fair piece from here."

"We got plenty of room, once you dump it," Baylor offered.

" 'Preciate it, but that *will* get the truce busted. It's risky enough I even visited your house. I'll camp north of here for the night."

"Comin' back?" Jesse asked.

"So far," Fargo replied, checking his cinches and latigos by feel in the near darkness, "I've been shot at, stabbed at, punched at, and had my horse stole. It's only going to get worse. I say live and let live, but my hand's been forced and now there's no turning back. It's fight or show yellow, and damn straight I *will* be back."

Holding their horses to a trot in the hot darkness, Fargo and Cranky Man bore due north toward the Missouri border—not the most advisable route for travelers in this region—as Fargo reminded the Choctaw.

"Way I figure," Cranky Man explained after they'd dumped the Puke's body in a covert, "safest place to hole up is right in the middle of their own nests. That's where they figure they're the safest."

"That shines," Fargo agreed. "Speaking of safe . . . you *do* realize I'm not the safest man to ride with around here? By now assassins are laying for me everywhere. The attack could come any place, anytime."

"Think I'm stupid?" Cranky Man grumped. "Let 'em attack, it's their funeral."

"I've seen you with a knife, and you're some pumpkins," Fargo said. "How are you with a rifle?"

"Pretty good at fifty yards, useless at a hundred."

"Hmm . . . won't win turkey shoots, but that'll do for close-in fighting," Fargo decided. "How 'bout with a six-shooter?"

"Huh! Why you think I'm so good with a blade?"

Fargo shook his head. "Blade? Chief, there's hundreds of Border Ruffians roaming this area, and Jayhawkers too. Not to mention murdering trash like the Evans clan. You'd need a wagonload of knives and hours to throw them all."

"Hell, you think I mean to attack them? They can't kill me if they don't see me, Fargo. Best way to win a fight is to avoid it."

"Avoid it? Well, guess what," Fargo said through grim lips, pointing to a low ridge on their left. At least twenty riders were silhouetted against the rising moon. "They see you now. Good bet they found blood and know their man was killed. Here they come!"

With a bloodcurdling whoop, the riders spurred their mounts off the ridge, guns already blazing.

"Best get that knife out!" Fargo shouted scornfully as he kneed the Ovaro to a gallop.

"Go suck an egg, hair-face!" the Choctaw retorted, slapping his skewbald hard on the rump.

"Forget about heading toward your cave just now," Fargo ordered. "Not until we lose them. Bear down toward the bottom grass; less chance we'll lame our horses. More room to shake 'em, too."

Most of the bullets, at this distance, whistled wide of the two men. Now and then, however, a lucky shot whipped in closer, one even tagging Fargo's left stirrup. The Trailsman debated returning fire with the Henry, but dismissed the idea. This many pursuers would not be turned back by one shooter, and those bullets might well be needed, before long, in a last-stand defense.

"They're staying on us like heat rash!" Cranky Man called out, glancing over his left shoulder. His magic-pebble necklace rattled as it bounced.

"Three-railer!" Fargo warned, indicating a farmer's three-rail-high fence that loomed just ahead.

Fargo's warning was not a mere courtesy. A man who did not time things perfectly when his horse jumped a rail or ditch could end up damaging the family jewels—or worse. Fargo shifted his weight forward and flexed his muscles in case of trouble. The Ovaro, a veteran at reckless escapes, lowered his powerful hindquarters and sailed over flawlessly even as bullets whined around them.

Cranky Man's skewbald, however, caught the top rail with one hoof and the Choctaw went sailing ass over applecart.

"I saw the whole thing!" Fargo berated the shaken Indian, reining in and helping him to his feet. "It was your fault the horse didn't clear—you kept his head down, you fool. Then he barely hits on one hoof, and you're tossed. Weren't you braced?"

"For a peeler, I got a round ass when it comes to staying in the saddle," Cranky Man admitted, flinging himself aboard his uninjured horse. "And now our friends are even closer."

Fargo required no reminder. Riders thundered closer, whooping and yipping as they smelled blood. Orange muzzle streaks were unrelenting now, and chunks of old fence wood flew into Fargo's face.

"Gotta buy time," he decided. "At this range, the sheer amount of lead will cut us down as we run. Break out that dead Puke's repeating rifle. Don't bother aiming; just spray your shots until the magazine's empty. I'll be doing the same. Two of us might drive them to cover down, let us escape."

Fargo jerked the Henry from its saddle boot and blew a quick puff of air to clear blow sand from the ejector port. He had sixteen rounds in the tube magazine and planned to use them all. The attackers were dangerously close now, whipping their mounts to a lather.

"One request, Fargo," Cranky Man said. "If I get killed, make sure my horse is close by."

Fargo nodded, not bothering to ask why. No Indian wanted to die without a mount in the Land of Ghosts.

"Put at 'em!" Fargo ordered, and both men laid their rifle barrels on the top rail.

The double barrage of closely spaced shots had an almost immediate effect. Several men cried out, wounded, and two horses buckled to their front knees before toppling over, pinning their riders.

"*That's* medicine!" Cranky Man shouted, still working the lever of his New Haven Arms repeater.

"Then keep dosing 'em with pills!" Fargo urged. "The center's been broke, swing your fire to the left flank."

He jacked round after round into the Henry's chamber, feeling the stock slap his cheek each time he fired. With a clicking sound like a roulette wheel, B. Tyler Henry's new ejector mechanism spewed hot brass casings into the grass. Finally the hammer fell on an empty chamber. Fargo heard hot gun oil sizzling in the barrel.

Their enemy, momentarily in disarray, was falling back or seeking cover.

Fargo booted his rifle, then hit leather and stood up in the stirrups to see better. "We best break dust in a puffin' hurry," he warned Cranky Man. "We mighta broke the charge, but them scrappers from Missouri hang on like ticks. Especially if their 'commanders' want Skye Fargo planted quick."

Both men chucked their horses up to a gallop across the grassy river flats, a pale, full moon their only light. At first no one pursued, and Cranky Man loosed a piercing victory whoop.

"You worry like an old woman, Fargo," he goaded. "Let's head toward my cave and get outside of some grub."

"Care to invite them?" Fargo asked, hooking a thumb over his shoulder.

"Shit, piss, and corruption!" Cranky Man groaned between curses. Riders were clearly visible against the pale wafer of moon. "Here they come again!"

"Only about half this time," Fargo said. "But that's still ten well-armed killers. Thump that cayuse up full bore, let's see can we outrun them."

Fargo expected good bottom from the Ovaro, but Cranky Man's skewbald, too, pinned back his ears and held a strong gallop. When they pulled in to let their horses blow, Fargo again stood up in the stirrups to study the moonlit terrain behind them.

"Like goddamn sticky burrs," he muttered. "They aren't closing fast, but they're on us to stay. This keeps up, they'll run us to ground."

He glanced at both horses. Even the Ovaro was still blowing hard.

"We could keep running," Fargo reasoned aloud. "But what's the point? We just keep lathering our horses and leaving a trail."

"Yeah, you're right, Fargo, let's just surrender," Cranky Man barbed. "After all, white man, *you* can just join 'em as a sharpshooter. Old Cranky Man will be shot to wolf bait, but you—"

"Whack the cork," Fargo snapped at him. "If I want you shot I'll do it myself. Look."

Fargo pointed to a narrow draw just ahead of them. "We can't lose 'em, so we're gonna turn 'em back. There's no easy way around that draw, the sides are too steep. The grass inside is knee-high, but tinder dry."

"Sure, and if we fire it, it can't really spread—these walls surrounding us are almost all rock."

Fargo nodded. "But we best hurry—they're gaining on us."

Both men kneed their mounts forward into the draw.

"Cover me," Fargo ordered Cranky Man, swinging down from the saddle. "But change positions or they'll get a bead on your muzzle flash."

The Border Ruffians had begun firing again, a few of their shots ranging in close. Fargo had no time for anything fancy. With Cranky Man banging away at the enemy, he knelt every twenty feet or so to make a fire bundle—double handfuls of dead grass twisted into crude kindling. Using the matches in his oilskin pouch, he moved across the draw igniting the bundles.

"Hell, Fargo, we're too late!" Cranky Man shouted above the crackle of flames. "The bastards are knocking on the door!"

Fargo shucked out his Colt and used all six beans in the wheel to drive back the lead riders. However, more were pressing from behind.

Horses hated and feared fire, and when Cranky Man's mount began nervously sidestepping, Fargo shouted, "Clear the draw, you ugly red son! When you get on the other side, reload your rifle. Shoot *any*body who comes riding out on anything except my pinto."

Before the Choctaw could protest, Fargo slapped the skewbald hard and it bolted. Now, however, as lead thickened the air around him, Fargo faced a deadly dilemma. With the stiff wind, it was taking him too long to ignite those bundles. The draw was indeed burning, but with too many escape routes left for the attackers.

The Ovaro, too, was growing increasingly skittish as deepening flames reflected in his frightened eyes. Hooves pounded closer like rolling thunder, and a bullet tore through one edge of Fargo's buckskin shirt, giving it a sharp tug.

That bullet literally tore it for Fargo. Hating to sacrifice a good U.S. Army blanket, but knowing it was his only choice, Fargo pulled his bedroll loose from the cantle straps. He set it afire in the nearest patch of blaze, then began a wild ride through the draw, dragging the blazing wool blanket anywhere that was still not aflame.

His tenacious enemies, however, did not passively observe this action. Forced, by their rebelling mounts, to stop short of the flaming draw, the Pukes opened up with a vengeance against their well-lighted target.

Fargo, who had come to manhood in a hail of deadly lead, had faced down plenty of withering gunfire in his life. This close-range volley now, however, was among the most savage in his experience. Nor had he ever asked the Ovaro to surround himself with sawing, deadly flames for so long.

"Gee up, old warhorse!" Fargo shouted above the din of fire, gunshots, and shouted curses. He reined around north, toward the escape route Cranky Man had taken. A bullet grazed the Trailsman's left cheek, leaving a burning line of white-hot pain.

Fargo lowered his profile in the saddle and thumped the Ovaro up to a gallop. Erratic wind currents had closed the loop on Fargo's grassfire, and with a sinking heart he saw the last gap for escape turn into a flaming portal of death. The high, dry grass made excellent fuel, wind-whipped flames surging as high as twelve feet.

"Jump *through*, not at," Fargo urged quietly as the magnificent stallion once again made his will one with Fargo's.

"You can do it, Fargo!" Cranky Man's voice urged from somewhere beyond the smoke and flames. "C'mon, you ballsy white devil, cheat the Reaper one more time!"

Even Fargo, no stranger to the reality of hard death, would rather die in any manner but the excruciating agony of fire. Jumping high enough was one thing; if the Ovaro couldn't also make the distance, they'd land smack in the flames.

"Now!" he shouted when the heat was so close it dried the film on his eyeballs. For extra measure, Fargo leaned forward to bite the Ovaro's tender ear.

The stallion, motivated by both fear and rage, lowered his hindquarters and leaped, man and horse soaring through the air. Smoke choked Fargo's throat and eyes, heat licked at his legs, and then—in a heartbeat—they were both safe.

Now that he knew his master was safe, the irritated stallion bucked Fargo off to teach him a lesson about ear biting. Fargo landed hard on his ass, and the pain was pure pleasure. Only living men felt pain . . .

Cranky Man seemed astounded by the escape. "I had you for a gone coon, Fargo. I guess some men are just too contrary to die."

"Helps to have a good horse," Fargo assured him, climbing to his feet. "But this ain't no time to recite our coups. Soon as that fire burns down, those shitheels will be dogging us. Now's the time to hook back around to your cave and that grub you mentioned. I've seen some double-rough gangs in my time, old son, but these Border Ruffians win the prize for being bloodthirsty sons of bitches."

7

Fargo and Cranky Man, no longer being pursued, rode along a brushy ridge in northwest Arkansas near the southern Missouri border. A few remaining lights blazed a soft halo over the crossroads settlement of Lead Hill.

The Ovaro started, and Fargo strained his ears. "The hell was that? Sounded almost like a wildcat."

"Wild dog," Cranky Man corrected him. "They're a danger in these river bluffs east of Lead Hill. One of the big betting sports around here is dog fighting, and plenty of mean curs escape. Plus the drought forces people out and they abandon their dogs. They form wild packs in the hills. Damn hellhounds."

"You ever ride into town?" he asked the half blood, still watching Lead Hill.

Cranky Man gave that one a hoot. "I thought you already learned how friendly Lead Hill *ain't*. Christ, Fargo, even a white stranger is jugged for vagrancy. They'd skin my half-breed hide and feed me to the hogs. The Evans clan controls that town, which means the Pukes do, too. It's rare for a week to pass without another killing at the Three Sisters saloon."

"Good place for a sane man to avoid," Fargo agreed, knowing he would soon be visiting that grogshop himself— a visit he intended to be long remembered.

"Here," Cranky Man said, reining into the trees and bushes beside the trail.

At first, to Fargo, the Choctaw was simply swallowed up by the dense cover. Then he saw a narrow path leading away from the main trail. Soon, dense overhead branches forced them to dismount and lead their horses.

The cave entrance, though a foot taller than Fargo, was ingeniously hidden behind a willow copse.

"Take your horse right inside," Cranky Man called back. "There's a spring-fed pool of cold water, and the air's cooler."

At first, even with Fargo's sharp night vision, the cave was darker than the inside of a boot. Then Cranky Man lit a few crude torches, and the place lost its hole-to-nowhere look. Buffalo robes were spread out here and there to soften the cold dirt floor, and upended packing crates served as chairs.

After the Ovaro had tanked up at the pool, Fargo stripped him of tack, curried the dried sweat off him, and gave the stallion a vigorous rubdown with a feed sack.

"What about your horse?" Fargo demanded. So far Cranky Man had not even loosened the skewbald's buffalo-hide saddle.

"That spavined nag?" Cranky Man retorted, busy wrestling the cork out of a jug of potato whiskey. "That tub of glue is lucky I ain't shot him by now."

"Spavined, my ass. That animal gave good service tonight."

Fargo pried open the horse's mouth and studied the inside. "Tub of glue!" he exclaimed. "This horse is six years old, at most. Plenty of good use left."

Cranky Man sat cross-legged on a buffalo robe, nursing

his jug. Fargo stared at him, those lake blue eyes puzzling things out.

"Cranky Man," he finally said, "I'm willing to believe you were once a horse peeler like the Tutt boy said, round ass or not. But I've never yet met a man who breaks green horses to leather and yet treats a horse like you do. Which means you now have a new way of feeding your face."

Now that his eyes were better accustomed to the light, Fargo noticed heaps of household items pushed back into the shadows—everything from canned food to patent medicines and bolts of expensive cloth.

"Opening a mercantile?" Fargo said sarcastically.

Cranky Man frowned, but said nothing when Fargo opened one of the Choctaw's buckskin panniers and reached inside. He pulled out a jimmy and stared at the hooded eyes of Cranky Man. "Horse peeler, huh? This is used to force open doors."

Cranky Man took a swig, then shuddered—potato whiskey was rough stuff. "Ah, you've seen the elephant, Fargo, you're a man of the world. You know how it is."

"What the *hell*?" This time Fargo's hand emerged holding one of the most illegal possessions in the nation, a barkey. It was a skeleton key shaft with a slot to hold four different bits. Given the crude locks of the day, a bar-key could open all but a few.

"I'm not the law," Fargo said, "and you saved my life. So we'll call it square and skip the wrong of it. But now I understand the 'rash of sneak-thievery' Sheriff Hollis mentioned. You get caught with this, it's the knot for sure. White man, red man, won't matter."

"I know," Cranky Man admitted. "But I'm trapped, Fargo. Hell, I grew up with the rest of my people in Mississippi. I liked it, all of it: the lazy heat, the gator hunts, the cypress and tupelo swamps. So after we were forced west to the Nations, naturally my people huddled up close as we could get to the eastern border of the rez."

"Seemed more like your native South," Fargo finished for him. "And of course that put you within easy reach of these Arkansas settlements. Not like Mississippi, maybe, but at least you don't have to answer roll calls and eat government pork."

Cranky Man nodded. "You got something to say about that?" he demanded gruffly.

"Only this—I *won't* let you hang for having a bar-key. You won't even get a trial."

Fargo stepped outside the cave and tossed the key far off into the tangled growth.

"Bastard," Cranky Man said without heat when he returned. "Whiskey?"

Fargo laid the jug on his shoulder and tipped out a few swallows, swearing aloud as it burned like coals in his empty belly. "Where's that food you promised?"

"Good beans in them cans near your foot. I don't bother heatin' 'em."

Fargo was hungry enough to agree. He pried a can open with the narrow point of his Arkansas toothpick. While he worked, he noticed that Cranky Man's left little finger had been cut off at the second joint.

"Dead wife," the half blood explained, seeing Fargo look at it. "I missed her, so I cut it off with a hatchet."

Fargo nodded, knowing that self-mutilation to express grief was a widespread custom among many tribes. This loss of his wife also helped explain Cranky Man's bitter cynicism. The loss of a good woman was often too much for a man to bear.

"What can it matter now?" Cranky Man said brusquely. "Much snow has fallen since then. The past is a dead thing and should be left alone."

Fargo spooned more beans into his mouth, letting the topic die. Clearly the Choctaw wanted no part of those earlier memories, and Fargo knew exactly how that felt.

However, Cranky Man's moods changed in a few heartbeats. He slanted a sly glance toward Fargo. "Now Mary Lou Tutt . . . *that* girl's a huckleberry above a persimmon, huh?"

" 'Pears to be," Fargo said evasively.

Cranky Man laughed so hard he almost dropped the whiskey. "Fargo, don't try that discreet gentleman shit *here*. You had a fine time going off into the bushes with Mary Lou earlier today."

Fargo set the can down. "You watched, you filthy old goat?"

"I had to, it was so damn funny. Why do you white-skins

waste time rubbing your mouths together? Your *mouths*!" Cranky Man shuddered at the depravity. "Now a red man, he just mounts his squaw, bulls her in fine style, grunts when he is done and goes to sleep. You, Trailsman, have much to learn."

"That's not what the ladies tell me, including the Indian gals."

Cranky Man looked genuinely puzzled. "The ladies? Who cares what *they* think?"

Fargo grinned. "To each his own, chief. But you ever spy on me again and I'll have your guts for garters."

The Choctaw walked back into the shadows and returned with a brand-new U.S. Army blanket.

"You'll need a replacement for the one you burned up," Cranky Man said. "You too proud to use a swiped blanket?"

"Not if I didn't steal it," Fargo replied, accepting it.

Fargo's thoughts, however, were back on that crucial hill located on Evans property. The same hill where he and Jesse Tutt had barely saved their own hides in a battle with Border Ruffians. Fargo had been on the hill and had some ideas where to search for Devil's Mouth, the supposed secret cavern used by Pukes.

Fargo's aggressive instincts urged him to find that cave quickly, just as one might rout out a snake den. Those same instincts urged him that Cranky Man, for all his dissolution and cynicism, was the perfect killer to take with him.

"You ain't got much use for Langston Evans and his clan, I take it?" Fargo asked.

"What, the Big Boss? Why the hell would I? True, I break into houses. But those sons of bitches are woman and child killers, Fargo. There's some shit a man can't scrape off his boots."

"Glad to hear it," Fargo said. "Because if the Evans clan goes under, so will the Pukes they hide. And you and me, old son, are going to bring 'em to ruination, starting tomorrow by exposing Devil's Mouth."

Cranky Man flopped onto a buffalo robe, laughing until his eyes streamed tears. "*Two* men taking on the Border Ruffians? Fargo, you ever heard of a fart in a hurricane?"

"That's the point—no one notices a fart in a hurricane. I never said we'd plant the whole bunch in one battle, you

60

chucklehead. But if we can break one axle, the whole wagon grinds to a halt."

Cranky Man shook his head. "You been mule-kicked, Fargo. Plumb loco. Boy, you need to pull stakes and get outta here. You thumped all over Clay Evans and you've killed their Border Ruffian pals. Every place you go in Arkansas, gun sights will be notched on you."

Fargo, picking his teeth with a twig, shrugged one shoulder. "Don't matter. These old boys pushed things too far when they stole my horse and tossed lead at me. Now it's root hog or die. I mean to teach these flea-bit sons of bitches some manners, but I'll need a good man like you to side me."

For a moment, pride flitted across the half blood's homely, angular face. "Good man, huh? Well . . . I think you're crazy to do this, Fargo, but half of courage is craziness. We're both already dead, but sure, I'll help you find Devil's Mouth."

Langston Evans was in a fine pucker, his aristocratic face tight with rage. Normally, by this late hour, the house would be silent as a graveyard. At the moment, however, the double parlor was again crammed full as it had been earlier that day.

"Once wasn't enough, was it?" he demanded, staring at the dour-faced men filling the sofa and wing chairs. "*Twice*, in one day, Fargo slips from your grip like a greased weasel. It's got me powerful wrathy, boys. Jimbo, I expect my own whelps to act like squeamish twats, but *you* I had some faith in."

Jimbo Powers, commander of the local Border Ruffians, had a hard face made harder by a spade beard. He wore the plumed hat and butternut clothing of his "army."

"The hell could I do, Langston? The bastard lit a fire—"

Langston shook his thick silver mane like an angry lion. "Never mind the damn excuses, all of you! I want Fargo cold as a wagon tire, and he better be killed damn soon. Do you ken the loss of income we'll all suffer if he finds that cave? Right now we're selling priddy near fifty horses *a month* to the Border Ruffians—ask Jimbo. But only on account we also have an excellent sanctuary to lure the men over the border."

"Fargo's a hired killer brung in by the Jayhawkers," Clay Evans insisted to his father. "He ain't here to ruin our business. He's here to kill Jimbo and, most likely, us Evans men."

Maw-maw Evans, rocking in her chair as she darned socks, loosed a harsh bark of laughter. "Clay, when a snake crawls 'tween your sheets, who in shit-ass hell cares *why* it's there? Boy, your pa is right as rain—douse Fargo's light, and mighty damn soon."

"Ain't just Fargo, either," Langston Evans reminded them. "As a fighter, old Joshua Tutt has hung up his fiddle. But both of his male whelps are in this fight, too."

Maw-maw chuckled. "Now, as to them boys . . . won't be no big problem to get them out of the mix, ain't that right, Hollis?"

Sheriff Hollis Maitland, Lead Hill's poor excuse for a peace officer, felt so uncomfortable about being here that he stood alone in front of the cold fireplace, looking even older than his fifty years.

"How's that, Miz Evans?" he said, face puzzled.

"I think you take my meaning," she assured him. "Just act like you own a pair. There's going to be a terrible crime soon, a *hanging* crime, and the evidence will point to Baylor Tutt. No more backing and filling, hear? It'll be your job to lock him up until the circuit judge gets to Lead Hill."

Hollis shrugged. He had to walk on eggs here— Maw-maw was the biggest toad in the puddle when it came to planning violent crimes.

"The Tutts are considered big bugs hereabouts," he pointed out. " 'Sides, I've never been a party to using the law to hang an innocent man."

When angry, Maw-maw Evans had a deep voice for a woman and she used it now. "Balls, you goddamn worm! *No* Tutt male is innocent, they all require killing. Scooter?"

"Yeah, Aunt Mattie?" Scooter Evans, his buckshot-riddled face a patchwork of sticking plaster, sat in a side chair scowling blue murder. Bear grease controlled his unruly red hair. The big brute wanted to kill Skye Fargo with an intensity like hell thirst.

"This chickenshit star packer of ourn," Maw-maw told her nephew, "has been drawing wages from us for months. Yet he let Fargo go when he had a chance to kill the meddling bastard. Me 'n' your Uncle Langston, we're powerful tired of feedin' a mule that won't plow. If Hollis here don't jug Baylor, after the horrible crime coming up, then I want you to geld him like the sister-boy he is, hear me?"

Scooter aimed his beady, insane eyes at the sheriff. "You mean *really* geld him?"

"Snip snip," she assured him. "And then pin his balls right under that badge on his vest."

Scooter's crooked grin was like bent wire. "Yes, ma'am. Be a puredee pleasure."

When the pale, shaken sheriff was dismissed, Langston Evans produced a jug of his own moonshine.

"Hey, Maw-maw," Dobie said, "what terrible crime is coming up?"

"Never you mind, boy." Maw-maw glanced at Scooter and winked. "It's in good hands."

"I still say all this shit oughter be avoided," oldest brother Clay said. "Me, Dobie, Scooter, and a few of Jimbo's boys should just attack the house, kill every Tutt."

"That still leaves Fargo," Langston reminded his son. "And the federal law dogs might nose into it. Comes down to it, we'll swarm down on the Tutt house. But I kallate we won't need to, not if we can kill Fargo."

"Don't forget my men are still after him," Jimbo Powers spoke up. "We bollixed the job today, no question. But we're good at flushing game, and even Fargo can't make himself invisible."

"Then you best do it afore that bullion coach rolls through here in a couple days," old man Evans advised. "Even if Ma's plan for framing Baylor works, Fargo has a way of showing up at the worst damn time. Not only will he prevent the holdup, he'll ruin our chance to lay the crime on Jesse Tutt."

"Get him while he's takin' a crap," Maw-maw repeated her sage advice. "Pants roping the ankles, mind gone lazy, gun laid aside so he can wipe his ass. Like shootin' a can off a fence."

8

"Lands, what a gorgeous day!" Holly Nearhood exclaimed.

The seamstress from Lead Hill was a tall, attractive brunette in a white walking dress. She loitered along the trail to gaze at the few wildflowers that had beaten the drought. It was around midmorning and Holly carried a long box under her arm. Mary Lou Tutt, Holly told herself, was going to dance for joy when she saw her new gown.

Clay and Dobie Evans had passed Holly earlier, and her heart had leaped into her throat. Usually those two talked filth to her. This morning, however, they merely averted their eyes.

"That's some strange," Holly muttered as she strolled along, enjoying the hill country where she'd been born and raised. "Since when did *them* two turn shy?"

About two miles from the Tutt farm, Holly was forced off the trail by a huge mercantile caravan. Plenty were now being organized in Arkansas and heading west to supply the towns, forts, and mining camps.

Holly dreamed about going west and getting rich in the millinery trade—all women needed hats. Maybe Omaha or even San Francisco. She'd never meet a suitable husband here, in a town only a stone's throw from the explosive Missouri border. A veteran army scout once told Holly that Missouri and Kansas were the most violent and dangerous places in the West, period. She knew this part of Arkansas got its share, too, and Holly planned to cut loose from Lead Hill the moment she had enough money saved. Then—

"Purdy day, huh?"

Holly cried out, the unexpected voice frightened her so. She watched Scooter Evans emerge from a clump of bushes to the right of the trail. The big, barrel-chested redhead's face was covered with sticking plaster.

"I ast you a polite goddamn question, high-toned woman," Scooter growled. "I guess you druther eat dog shit than talk to me, hey?"

That was true enough, but Holly was too shocked to even understand the crazy monster's talk. When she tried to edge away, Scooter grabbed her arm in a grip like a steel trap. He slapped her so hard that Holly's teeth clacked like dice and her ears were left ringing. A second, harder slap addled her thoughts.

"Yeah, you fart through silk, don'tcha?" he hissed as he dragged the stunned woman farther up the slope and into the screening timber. "Well, silky-satin slut, guess what? I'm gonna poke you a new one. And when I'm done makin' you see God, I'm gonna *send* you to Him."

Holly tried to beg for her life, but Scooter grew uglier and uglier as he ripped her pantaloons off and lust got him in its grip. He was brutal, especially when it became clear he was having trouble reaching climax. After he finally did, Holly looked as if she'd been beaten by drunken miners.

The new gown had fallen out of its box and lay close beside Holly in the grass. Her heart became a fist of ice when Scooter pulled out a steel-bladed knife with a leather-wrapped hilt. Both edges of the ten-inch blade glinted cruelly, honed to a lethal sharpness. The initials B. T. were burned into the leather.

"Scooter, *no!*" she begged. Holly tried to scootch away, but the big brute had straddled her.

"Shush, girl, shush," he said in a soothing voice even as he opened Holly's abdomen up with one fast swipe of the knife. Blood rapidly pooled on her stomach, and then ran in rivulets into the gown.

Holly was beyond screaming now. The excruciating fire in her abdomen, the horrid sound of her blood spurting out, meant death was only moments away. Even so, the sick monster from the lowest depths of hell wasn't through with her quite yet.

Scooter stood up, and closed his fly, and then picked up his rifle musket. He used his teeth to tear open a paper cartridge containing powder and ball.

"Scooter . . . why? You've already . . . killed me," Holly

managed between breathless gasps. Though badly cut, she secretly prayed someone might find her in time—if he left. "Please just leave and . . . let me die in peace."

Scooter poured the powder down the barrel and pushed in the bullet with his thumb. He drew the ramrod and pushed the projectile home.

"Can't be did, girl. I want you dead afore I leave, and you could last an hour or more."

Scooter pulled back the rifle musket's hammer and placed a percussion cap on the nib beneath the hammer.

"*No*, Scooter!" Holly cried when the sadistic madman brought the end of the muzzle to the exact center of her forehead.

"Yes," he said softly as he pulled the trigger, blasting away much of her head.

Scooter smiled as he deliberately left the knife lying beside the bloody body. He himself had picked it up when Baylor Tutt lost it during a fistfight at the Three Sisters saloon. With Sheriff Maitland eating at the Evans' trough, Baylor Tutt was now a gone coon.

Unless . . . as Scooter headed toward his hidden horse, the bearded, steel-jawed image of Skye Fargo returned to his mind. With that image came the memory of Fargo using a trick shot to explode Scooter's own shotgun in his face.

"Got a reckoning comin', you smug son of a bitch," Scooter muttered. "You're gonna wish you'd died as a child."

The American folk migration was in full swing, and Fargo and Cranky Man spotted two caravans and several lone drummers leading pack animals, during their first hour in the saddle, scouting the hills and bluffs around the suspected location of Devil's Mouth. The night before, thanks to Cranky Man's cave, Fargo had slept six hours—the most he'd ever slept outside of a hotel bed.

"Makes me puke," Cranky Man snarled, watching one of the wagon caravans cross the drought-stunted grass of a valley below. "The white man was one of the All-maker's only mistakes."

Fargo, busy watching the ambush points closer to hand, snorted. "Ahh . . . just when did the All-maker admit that mistake to you? And while he spoke in your ear, did he add anything about drunk, grumpy Choctaws who smell like a bear's den and steal from people's houses?"

Cranky Man dismissed him with a careless wave. Both men had dismounted to water their horses in a streamlet.

"Hear that?" Cranky Man asked.

Fargo nodded. Someone in the distant caravan was playing a banjo, which Fargo heard along the trail far more often than guitars. An instrument invented by American slaves, he mused, being used in the quest for freedom. These were cockeyed times, all right.

"You're pretty sure you know the right hill?" Cranky Man asked, removing his greasy flap hat and swiping at his sweaty brow with a bandanna.

"Yep. It's that high, long one with all the pine growth." Fargo pointed straight across the yellow-brown valley floor.

"Makes sense," Cranky Man conceded. "That's on Evans land."

"And why else," Fargo wondered aloud, "would Border Ruffians be riding up there so often—usually right after a bank heist or train robbery?"

Cranky Man pointed at the red burn on Fargo's left cheek where a Puke bullet had grazed it the night before.

"Fargo, you got the balls of a stud bull, but your brain is more the size of a woodpecker's. That crease is a whatchacallit, an omen. Just forget about this cave and haul your butt back out west. This ain't your fight."

"It's every good man's fight," Fargo said as he hit a stirrup and swung up into leather. "Besides, it's personal. Speaking of that . . . I've already met the two Evans boys and their pig-eyed cousin Scooter. You broke horses for them—what's the old man like?"

"Langston? 'Bout what you'd expect in a crazy, murdering bastard who's power hungry. Like plenty around here he's one a them eagle-screamers. Thinks everybody oughta be killed to expand the country—for slavery. I hear his family's had money since it was called wampum—dirty, bloody money. But they pretend to have Methodist feet."

Fargo nodded, catching the reference. People of that day and place were either dancers or had "Methodist feet," and society formed around the two groups.

"You ask me," Cranky Man added, "it's Langston's damned flint-hearted wife, Matilda, who rules the roost. Maw-maw, they call her. Damned hell hag is what she is."

Some distance ahead, Fargo heard the snarling of a dog. He knocked the rawhide thong off the Colt's hammer and loosened the six-shooter in its holster.

"The Tutts are better liked in this area," Cranky Man said, "but that damn scheming Evans bunch have got lick-fingers everywhere, including Hollis Maitland."

"I know," Fargo replied. "I'm watchin' for 'em now."

"For a long time," Cranky Man said, "this Tutt-Evans feud paced along slow. Now it looks like the Evans bunch are making a push to wipe out the Tutts and grab their land."

"They want to be on it if and when the Homestead Act passes," Fargo surmised. "According to Dame Rumor, it could be passed anytime now."

"What's the Homestead Act?"

Fargo started to reply, but more snarling—much closer at hand—made him rein in.

"Just wild dogs," Cranky Man remarked idly. "Steer clear and we'll be all right."

"No," Fargo said, studying the signs in the trail. "This is more than wild dogs."

He pointed at the ground. "I been noticing a fresh set of human footprints for at least a mile now. A woman, judging from the shape of the sole. They stop here. Look up the slope, and you can see furrows where she dragged her heels. She was dragged up."

"Oh, hell," Cranky Man said. "She was attacked?"

Fargo nodded, swinging down and pulling his Henry from its saddle boot. "Looks that way. And judging from those snarls, we're gonna find her close by."

Fargo's first fear was for Mary Lou. As the two men worked their way up the slope, the snarling grew louder and more vicious. Fargo had his Colt to hand, Cranky Man his New Haven Arms repeating rifle.

"Jesus," Fargo said in a whisper, pushing aside a tree branch. A dead woman lay in the grass of a little clearing, skirts hiked up over her hips. She was covered with a shifting blanket of blue-black, buzzing flies. Two wild curs were snapping at each other over possession of the body.

One bullet sent both dogs streaking to deeper cover.

"Know her?" Cranky Man asked.

"Know who she was," Fargo said, his mouth grim with angry determination. He was a mild man and did not take offense easily. Once the Trailsman got that squint in his eyes, however, there was usually a funeral. "But I never met her."

With the scuffed toe of his boot he touched the blood-soaked gown beside her. "She's the seamstress from Lead Hill. Holly somebody. I got a glimpse of her yesterday. Most likely she was taking that gown out to Mary Lou Tutt."

"See the initials on that knife?" Cranky Man asked.

Fargo had indeed, and he suspected a frame-up. He would not, however, remove any evidence, planted or not.

Cranky Man asked, "Think Baylor coulda done it?"

"I just met him yesterday," Fargo said. "He seems like a good man. But then, so do plenty of killers. Whoever it was," he vowed, "I'll fix his flint."

"What now? Hollis Maitland ain't no kind of sheriff."

"No," Fargo agreed. "But it might be interesting to see how he reacts to this. We'll leave that knife right where it is."

For Fargo, until now, this layover in Arkansas was mostly personal. But when a woman or child was killed, *every* man became the sheriff.

Fargo returned to the Ovaro, took his groundsheet out from the cantle straps, and returned to cover Holly's body.

"I don't dare haul the body into Lead Hill," Fargo mused aloud. "We might hafta escape from Border Ruffians at any moment, and she'll weight my stallion down."

"And I can't show my face anywhere," Cranky Man pointed out. "A half-breed Choctaw is still a Choctaw. I'd be arrested for jumping the rez."

Fargo nodded, hitting leather. "Do me a favor. Stay here with the body until you hear me and Maitland coming down the trail. Then you can just slip off over the crown of the hill."

Cranky Man started to object, then glanced toward the body. His usual wrinkled frown was replaced by deep sympathy. "I'll do it," he agreed. "Guess finding that cave'll have to wait, uh?"

"It will," Fargo agreed, kneeing his Ovaro north toward Lead Hill. "But not for long."

Despite everything that was playing on his mind, Fargo kept a weary eye out during the short ride into Lead Hill. Twice he spotted groups of patrolling riders, clad in butternut, before they spotted him, reining in to hide until they passed. All this vigilance, however, couldn't drive from his mind the image of Holly's fly-carpeted body.

"You fiend-begotten wretch," he muttered aloud. "Whoever you are."

It was only around noon, but Lead Hill—or at least, the Three Sisters saloon—was going great guns when Fargo rode in. At least a dozen horses, bridles dropped, were lined up at the hitching post.

Fargo liked to take care of practical matters first. He drew rein at Romer Wiltz's livery to purchase a bag of oats for the Ovaro.

"You headed into the Sisters?" the barrel-built Romer asked while Fargo tied the oats behind his cantle.

Fargo glanced out the wide double doors and across the dusty street at the ramshackle saloon. "I might be at that," he replied.

"It's chock-full of Pukes," Romer warned. "I mention that only because you and Clay Evans done some huggin'. And stay away from the strumpets who ply their trade there. They all got the French pox."

He meant syphilis. Fargo said, "I take it you found out the hard way?"

Romer gave a rueful nod and held out his right hand. "Next time I get the urge, it's the poor man's harem for me."

"Nothing wrong with a man holding his own," Fargo agreed, and both men laughed.

However, the levity passed quickly, and Fargo considered his options. He had intended to search out Hollis Maitland next. However, the Trailsman was in a dangerous mood since discovering Holly's body, and he was tired of being on the defensive. So he tied off his Ovaro in front of the saloon and slid the Henry from its scabbard. Boot heels thumping on the boardwalk out front, he slapped open the batwings and stepped into the dark, smoky, noisy interior.

It was a crude groggery more than a full-blown saloon. The bar was just a long, thick plank set across barrels. The tables were upended packing crates, the chairs just stools or empty kegs. Brass cuspidors were placed everywhere, but as usual out west, most men used the floor instead.

The moment the tall, buckskin-clad, rifle-toting figure pushed into the place, the men crowding the tables fell silent. Despite all the hostility in the air, a middle-aged bartender wearing oilcloth sleeve covers greeted the stranger cordially. "Hallo, old hoss! I've got bad whiskey and middling-good beer, though it's warm."

"Beer," Fargo decided, aware of all the eyes dividing his back into kill zones.

The bartender drew a mug of beer, suds billowing, and thumped it down in front of Fargo. "Got a smart choice of cigars, too," the barkeep said, offering a box filled with a dozen different types. Fargo selected a skinny black Mexican smoke.

"Plank your cash, friend," the barkeep told Fargo. "Two bits for the beer, two more for the smoke."

Fargo slapped fifty cents onto the counter. He knew trouble was coming, and now it arrived.

"Boys, is that a whiff of skunk I smell?" said a reedy voice behind him.

Laughter bubbled through the building. Fargo revolved slowly around. The apparent speaker was a heavyset man with weather-rawed skin.

"Mister," Fargo warned him, "you're sniffing the wrong dog's butt."

Fargo knew, the second he turned around, that the Puke shitheel was holding a gun hidden under the table. By the unwritten code, a firearm drawn in a saloon showed clear intent to kill. As if it were spring-loaded, the Henry swung up into Fargo's two-handed grip and he plugged the Border Ruffian dead center in the forehead.

The Puke flopped forward onto the table, tipping over his friends' glasses. His cocked six-gun, a .36 Colt Navy, hit the plank floor and detonated. A man at the next table screamed when the bullet struck his groin.

"Sometime earlier today," Fargo announced in a tone that brooked no sass, "the seamstress from Lead Hill was raped and murdered. My name is Skye Fargo, and I will

71

not abide a woman killer. Either the killer gets turned over to me, or I start killing every Puke son of a bitch I see."

Fargo lowered the Henry's still-smoking muzzle. "Anybody don't like it, skin your barking irons and let's get thrashing."

A good aim and a steady hand under fire—Fargo knew this was more crucial than being the first to get off several quick shots. His trouble-seeking eyes flicked from man to man, inviting each to die.

"How in blue blazes do you know it was one of us done it?" a voice demanded.

"I don't," Fargo admitted. "But birds of a feather and all that. I'd bet my horse you know who did it."

"There's only one a him, boys," a voice from the back tried to rally the others.

"Yeah, he can't get us all!"

However, a bearded man seated close to Fargo seemed impressed. "Wouldjus all just shut your damn mouths?" he called out in warning. "Dampen your powder, boys. I know of this hombre, and he's a good man to let alone."

On that recommendation, Fargo backed cautiously out, finger curled around the Henry's trigger. Evidently, the sound of his shot had alerted Hollis Maitland. The silver-haired sheriff hurried across the dusty clearing, his Smith & Wesson drawn.

"Shoulda knowed you'd be in the mix, Fargo," he greeted the Trailsman. "Self-defense, of course?"

Fargo sent him a nervy little grin. Like Maitland, he held his weapon at the ready, but muzzle down. "Of course. You'll find him resting quietly inside. Such stupidity is refreshing—the fool had a cocked revolver aimed at me under the table."

"I tend to b'lieve you," Maitland conceded. "If you murdered a Puke in cold blood, they'd've perforated you. You wait right here while I talk to witnesses."

"Witnesses?" Fargo gave that a hoot. "Just ask the bartender. He saw the whole thing."

Maitland disappeared inside. A Puke came running out and crossed to the undertaker's parlor. Fargo kept his back to a wall and his Henry cocked.

"You told the straight truth, Fargo," Maitland said when he emerged again. "Every Puke in there swears it's murder.

But Jack, that's the barkeep, supports your story. And I've knowed him nigh onto twenty years." Maitland leathered his shooter. "Fargo, I like you, but you're six sorts of trouble. Why'n't you just drift on outta here?"

"Can't, at the moment. Best saddle your horse and come with me."

"Why?"

"Because," Fargo told him, "there *was* a murder today, a real one. And I'm taking you to the body."

9

Hollis Maitland's weathered face struggled to hold its composure when Fargo pulled back his canvas groundsheet, exposing the savagely murdered woman beneath it.

"Yeah, that's Holly Nearhood," he said in a gruff tone.

"You don't seem all that surprised to learn it," Fargo said.

"Killings around here are no surprise, Fargo. But I admit it rocks me back on my heels to discover it's Holly."

Fargo, knowing Maitland was paid off by the pro-Border Ruffians Evans clan, watched the law officer's face and manner closely. The horror in his eyes seemed mixed with guilt.

"And look right there," Maitland added, gingerly touching the steel-bladed knife with the toe of his boot. "Right there is Baylor Tutt's knife. I've seen it on him many times."

"Tell me, Sheriff. If you raped and killed a woman, would you leave a knife, with your initials on it, beside the body? Or does that sound plain stupid?"

"Course I wouldn't," Maitland replied. "But men make stupid mistakes in the heat of a crime."

That was true enough, but Fargo didn't like the way

Maitland was refusing to even look around the area for signs. This all seemed too neat and planned. *He seems more scared than bent,* Fargo decided.

"One of the Evans boys did this," Fargo decided. "Either you help them frame Baylor, or they kill you. Right?"

"Christ, Fargo, at least pre*tend* you got more brains than a rabbit. Whoever done this was savage as a meat ax. Even the Evans boys ain't *this* sick and mean."

"The two brothers, you mean. But does that include their cousin, Scooter?"

Just hearing the name, Maitland's face paled. Fargo had puzzled it out by now. Not only did Scooter Evans almost surely kill Holly, he would be the one to kill Maitland if he rebelled. Mary Lou's words from yesterday surfaced in Fargo's memory: *I saw Scooter beat a horse to death with his bare fists.*

"Where you going?" Fargo demanded when the peace officer started downslope toward his horse.

"To send the undertaker out before predators attack the body," he called back. "Then I'm taking a posse out to arrest Baylor Tutt."

"Like hell you are."

Maitland sent him a cross-shoulder glance. "Why shouldn't I?"

"This ain't a miner's camp, Hollis, with vigilante law. You need at least one witness, not just a knife. And a witness that doesn't lick Langston Evans' boots, at that. This rule by hemp committee has no place in an organized state."

Maitland slowly, reluctantly nodded. "Maybe you got a point, Fargo. But I'll have to talk with Baylor, at least."

Fargo nodded. "Fair enough. Talk to him. But that man risked his life to save my horse, and I'll guarandamntee one thing: you railroad him to the gallows, and you'll by God answer to me."

Fargo had no intention of trusting Maitland. True, the man appeared to be a coerced puppet, not a willing player in the local crimes. However, a scared man was more unpredictable than a criminal, and Fargo didn't like surprises.

So he headed due south toward the Tutt farm.

"Fargo! Wait up!"

He slued around in the saddle and watched Cranky Man, on his dish-faced skewbald, emerge from the trees onto the trail.

"I hid close by while you and Maitland palavered," the Choctaw explained as his horse trotted up. "You're headed off to warn the Tutts, ain'tcha?"

Fargo nodded, kicking the Ovaro forward again. "Damn straight. This has got frame-up stamped all over it. And Maitland may *say* he won't arrest Baylor yet, but the truth is he goes over the range if he doesn't."

"Because of Scooter Evans." Cranky Man nodded. "If a white man asked me to describe the Wendigo, I'd tell him to look in Scooter's eyes. Ain't just him, though. The whole Evans clan are meaner than Satan with a sunburn."

Fargo had to agree based on what he'd seen. Especially Clay Evans, who Mary Lou swore had vowed to rape and kill her. *Well, now he's got me to kill first,* Fargo thought.

"They'll come tonight for Baylor," Cranky Man predicted. "Maitland and a bunch of 'special deputies' drawn from the Pukes. And Baylor will be dead before they get him to Lead Hill. They'll plug him in the back and claim he tried to escape."

"That rings right," Fargo conceded.

"The two boys, Baylor and Jesse, are stout fighters," Cranky Man volunteered. "The old man, Joshua, took a hard kick to the skull, but I've seen him handle a rifle with skill. Add me and you, that's five rifles to defend the house. Could be worse."

"You?" Fargo thumbed back his hat to stare at the half blood. "Why? You said the white man was the All-maker's only mistake."

Cranky Man scowled, then spit. "I still think so. But you coulda aired me out yesterday when you caught me in your saddlebags. Most white-skins would've. You ain't the *worst* man alive, Fargo."

" 'Preciate that ringing endorsement," Fargo said dryly.

"Sure, ride along. The extra gun may come in handy."

As the two men rode in and out from shade to bright sunlight, Fargo's slitted, mountain-lake eyes studied the terrain closely, looking for reflections, movement, smoke, or dust puffs.

"It's a damn landgrab," Fargo said, thinking aloud. "The

Evanses ain't part of the Puke bunch, not officially. But one hand is washing the other. They give the Pukes a hideout and fresh mounts, the Pukes do their dirty work for them. Including killing the Tutts and taking their section of rich bottomland."

Cranky Man nodded. "And now Skye Fargo has made himself target number one around here. Anyplace, anytime . . . might be an assassin behind any tree."

"That puts you in the crosshairs too, old son."

Cranky Man touched the magic pebbles strung around his neck. "These make bullets turn to sand."

Fargo grinned. "Yeah? Bullets into sand? Well, you were sure ducking and weaving last night when those Pukes put at us."

Cranky Man's trademark frown took over his clay-colored face. "Christ, Fargo, I 'magine even sand hurts when it hits you at full muzzle speed."

Fargo laughed and let it go. He hadn't eaten since gnawing on a heel of cold pone that morning in Cranky Man's cave hideout, and his stomach was growling. Fargo was hungry for good hump steak, but the buffalo no longer came this far east due to human settlement.

"I hear more dogs snarling," he remarked. "Sounds like it's coming from the direction of that big hill on the Evans property."

"The most dangerous animals in these parts," Cranky Man reminded him, "go on two legs, not four."

"Now and then," Fargo replied, "you say something sensible."

They rounded a turn, and the Tutt farm hove into view, the surrounding bottomland green with flourishing crops despite the serious drought.

"Oh *ho*. There's your little play-pretty," Cranky Man roweled Fargo.

Mary Lou Tutt did indeed look pretty in a cool white muslin dress and a straw hat sporting a gay blue ribbon. She had just stepped past the yard gate, a peck basket depending from one slim white arm.

"Skye!" she exclaimed as they rode near, relief washing over her face. "Laws, Mr. Buckskins! You worry a body half to death wondering if you're still among the living.

Last night you said you was going out to check on your horse—then you never came back."

She cast a curious, suspicious glance at Cranky Man. Her brothers knew him slightly, but Mary Lou had never seen him before.

Fargo dismounted from the left, or near, side, Cranky Man from the right—the Indian side.

"I'm just now heading into the woods to pick berries," Mary Lou told Fargo, those sloe eyes teasing him. "Sure could use some help."

"Sorry, little lady, I'm saving myself for marriage," Cranky Man replied in his flat tone, and Fargo had to force back a laugh when Mary Lou flushed pink to her earlobes.

"Right now," Fargo said gently, taking her shoulders, "I've got some bad news for you. Are your brothers home, especially Baylor?"

"Oh, lands," Mary Lou whispered. Out loud she added, "Jesse is mending harness in the barn, and Baylor is weeding the corn. I'll fetch 'em both."

There was an iron triangle on a pole in the side yard. Mary Lou rang it with an old pewter ladle while Fargo and Cranky Man led their horses into the pasturage out back, where Baylor's strawberry roan was grazing. Both mounts had been watered earlier. Fargo stripped the leather off his Ovaro and spread the sweat-drenched saddle blanket in the hot sun. He dried the stallion with a feed sack, then began quickly currying off the dried sweat.

By now Mary Lou, Baylor, and Jesse had gathered around him.

"Holly Nearhood was killed earlier today," he told them without preamble, and Mary Lou instantly burst into tears. The two brothers looked grim as pallbearers.

"Who done it?" Baylor demanded. "Holly was a lady from the ground up."

"According to the . . . evidence," Fargo replied, "it was you."

All three Tutts looked astonished. Baylor's eyes went smoky with rage. All were still too shocked to speak.

"She was on her way here with Mary Lou's new gown when she was raped, then cut bad and shot in the head," Fargo added. "A steel-bladed knife with a leather-wrapped haft was found beside her. The initials 'B. T.' were burned into the leather.''

"It's lying rubbish!'' Baylor snapped. "I lost that knife a while back in a scuffle at the Three Sisters."

"Course it's rubbish," Fargo assured him. "The Evans clan knows they can't grab this land while two strapping young bucks are protecting it. So they're counting on lynch law—local outrage over killing a woman will justify a quick necktie party. My gut tells me it was that sorry-ass Scooter Evans who did the dirty deed."

Jesse nodded, anger twisting his broad, smooth-shaven face. "The very man, Skye, although 'man' is a stretch. That low-crawling, godless reptile would shoot his own mother for snoring."

"Skye?" Mary Lou interjected. "If the murdering Evans bunch are out to railroad Baylor, won't they have to try it with Jesse, too?"

Fargo nodded, vigilant eyes to all sides. "Makes sense they will, Mary Lou. But right now we have to get ready for *this* fandango. Hollis Maitland claims he'll be talking to Baylor, but I doubt it. Since your place is hard to sneak up on by day, I predict Hollis and a bunch of Pukes will be visiting after dark to seize him."

"*We* have to get ready?" Baylor repeated. "Hell, this ain't none of your lookout, Skye."

The Trailsman shook his head. "A woman was brutally murdered, and it's my business now. Even this lazy, reprobate Choctaw here is ready to join the fight."

"Reprobate? Whatever that means, pitch it to hell, white man," Cranky Man fired back.

"Old Man Evans planned it slick," Baylor said. "We got a standing truce with them not to attack each other's house. But this will be Maitland and some jackleg 'deputies,' not the Evans boys, so's we can't retaliate."

"We'll have to see about that," Fargo said quietly. "Way I see it, a man should give as good as he gets."

Fargo pointed toward the big, split-log house. "Your place is two stories and sits on a piece of high ground. Should give an excellent view of the road and the surrounding terrain. Most often these cutthroat gangs operate under cover of darkness, but even so, for the rest of the day I recommend we keep a sentry topside."

Jesse had brought his long Kentucky rifle with him from the barn. He raised it up. "I'll take the first shift."

"Got a posthole digger?" Fargo asked Baylor.

The eldest Tutt boy nodded. "All our land is fenced, so we had to get one."

"Good, saves us some hard labor." Fargo, a veteran of several sieges, pointed toward the house. A wide expanse of ankle-high grass yard surrounded it. "These night riders all operate the same. They like to circle a house just like Indians will circle a wagon train. Riding fast, shooting hard, tightening the circle all the time. They tend to be drunk and reckless. We'll pepper that ground with holes. Don't take much to snap a horse's leg bone, which puts its rider out of the fight."

"I'll turn that ground into a prairie-dog town," Baylor vowed.

The little group had begun walking back toward the house. Friendly hounds thumped their tails on the ground, greeting Fargo and Cranky Man.

"Another thing," Fargo said. "If they can't shoot us out, they'll try to burn us out. We'll need water buckets in every room. Fill any container you can find."

They filed into the house. Old Joshua Tutt was fast asleep on a chintz-covered sofa in the parlor, snoring loud enough to wake snakes. Ma Tutt was back in the slope-off kitchen, cutting out biscuit rounds with a tin can. The old matriarch gave Fargo a friendly smile with her greeting, but slanted a suspicious glance at the heavyset, unkempt Choctaw.

"Don't you belong out west on a reservation, John?" she demanded, raising her voice as if shouting English loud enough made it clear to those who couldn't speak it.

"The name is Cranky Man, not John. And my people belong in Mississippi," he retorted. " 'Cept that we was run out by white thieves hiding behind lawyers. The Indian Removal Act, they called it."

"Don't you take that tone with—"

"Simmer down, Ma," Baylor chimed in. "Cranky Man is with Skye, and both of 'em are here to fight for us."

Baylor summed up the situation with Holly Nearhood, Ma Tutt's worn, wrinkled face creasing with new worries. A kettle of lard heating on the old Franklin stove began to bubble and pop. Fargo watched Ma Tutt pour the hot lard into a crock filled with hunks of freshly cooked meat. This way it would keep indefinitely and was far less trouble than salting the extra.

"It's a sin to Moses," Ma Tutt muttered when Baylor fell silent. "By hard work, and the Lord's grace, we survived this cussed drought. Now they're out to hang my boy, and poor Holly lies cold. With all them Pukes on the Evans side, what chance we got?"

"The victory doesn't usually go to the dirtiest side, ma'am," Fargo assured her. "Nor to the most numerous. It goes to the side with the most will to win."

By now Jesse had dragged out a ladder and scrambled up onto the shingled roof for sentry duty. Baylor, true to his word, had gone to work outside with the posthole digger. Fargo had Mary Lou give him and Cranky Man a quick tour of the house to see which windows and rooms were good for defense.

"This here's my room," she announced coyly, throwing open a door in the rear of the house. "That smell is from the kerosene."

She meant the four bowls of kerosene into which the legs of the bed had been set to ward off bedbugs.

Fargo took in the ruffled bedspread, lace curtains, and rose-patterned carpet. A painting called *Davy Crockett at the Alamo* hung over the narrow iron bedstead. Fargo grinned when he realized the attackers were not Mexican lancers but warpath Indians. "Nice room," he said.

"Gets a mite lonely," Mary Lou hinted, but it didn't get past Cranky Man.

"If you two'd like to be alone," he suggested in his dead-pan manner, "I can go outside and do Indian stuff."

Mary Lou flushed again, definitely not liking this unsavory looking savage in the greasy flap hat.

"I 'preciate what you're doing for my family, mister," she remarked from those perpetually pursed lips. "But you need some training in manners."

"No misdoubting that," Cranky Man agreed.

Fargo, busy checking the angle of fire from Mary Lou's two sash windows, laughed at her comment. "Hon, you'll teach cats to preach gospel before you civilize *that* 'civilized' Indian."

However, Cranky Man's manner suddenly changed when he saw a stack of old envelopes on the oak highboy. "*That's* medicine! Miss Mary Lou," he said politely, "can you spare any of those medicine bundles?"

When she realized he meant the envelopes, her pretty face went blank with confusion. But after Fargo explained that there was "power" in white man's calligraphy, she gave Cranky Man most of the envelopes. Now she and the Choctaw were newfound friends.

The house filled with delicious cooking odors while Fargo and Cranky Man finished their inspection. From a big rainwater cistern out back, the two men hauled in a plentiful supply of water for dousing flames—milk pails, empty kerosene cans, old gut bags made from buffalo bladders, every possible container was filled and strategically placed around the house. The Tutts also had an old tin washtub out back that Fargo dragged inside and filled to the brim.

A drumbeat of hooves out front sent Fargo's palm to the walnut grips of his Colt.

"Stand easy!" Jesse shouted down from the roof. "It's just Ron Shoemaker, the express rider."

All this activity had roused Joshua Tutt from his nap. Fargo carefully explained the new trouble looming about Baylor. The Trailsman could tell, from the old patriarch's fire-and-brimstone eyes and strong-featured face, that such news would have given him fits in the days before his head injury. Now, however, he merely shook his head like a man who'd been rooked at faro.

"For true?" he asked when Fargo fell silent. "Ain't it a case of the drizzling shits? I tell you, Mr. Fargold, Eastern capital is the enemy of the westering man."

Fargo and Cranky Man exchanged quick glances, the Choctaw rolling his eyes.

"That's true enough, sir," Fargo said. "But your troubles right now are closer to home. You—"

"It's them consarned railroad plutocrats," the old man insisted, not understanding the younger man. "Not only did their back-scratching cousins in congress give them huge tracts of prime land for next to nothing, but the railroads turned right around and sold much of that land for huge profits—booting the owners right off the first time they missed their taxes."

All this was dead-on, but irrelevant at the moment. Fargo smiled at the old man and gave it up as a bad job. Ma Tutt called everyone to dinner after Fargo had run a plate up to Jesse.

If Joshua Tutt had rules against eating with wild savages, he suspended them when Cranky Man shoved his stubby legs under the table.

"Crooked Man, is it?" he demanded as he speared a piece of hot cracklin' bread from a platter.

"Cranky Man," the Choctaw corrected him, busy shoveling stew into his mouth.

With every meal, Fargo had noticed, Cranky Man set a morsel aside for the spirits.

"I hope them ghosts you worship like fat and gristle," Fargo remarked quietly around a mouthful of food. "That's all you leave 'em."

"Mary Lou!" snapped Ma Tutt. Her daughter was holding one of the orphaned Tutt babies in her lap while she ate. "I've told you before, don't *never* rock a baby—you'll mess up his brain and turn him stupid."

"So, Mr. Crooked Man," Joshua continued, a mischievous glint in his eye. He waved an old copy of *Scientific American* in the air. "You red aborigines being experts on terrain and such . . . do you know when you call a rock a boulder?"

Cranky Man liked to eat in peace. He frowned at all the damn talk. "Hell, I don't know," he snapped irritably. "When it conks you on the head?"

Fargo and Baylor snorted at the same time.

"No!" Pa Tutt shouted victoriously. "Savvy red man, my sweet aunt! Listen to this: 'We call it a rock until it reaches ten inches in diameter. Then it is classified a boulder.' "

"Well, there you have it," Fargo remarked awkwardly, for the old man was now staring fixedly at him. "I'll never look at the West the same."

"If you're counting on that old fool to burn powder with us tonight," Cranky Man whispered to Fargo after dinner, "then you also believe you can write on water. *His* glory days are smoke behind him now."

Fargo nodded reluctant agreement. "Even if he can still shoot plumb, he won't have sense enough to cover down."

Baylor joined them in the parlor before he went back to digging holes. He carried a double-barreled shotgun.

"My old cap and ball," he told Skye, meaning the dragoon pistol in his belt, "is accurate and will knock a man into the middle of next week. But it needs recharging after every shot, so I'll be totin' this smoke pole, too. It only fires twenty-gauge bird shot, though."

Fargo examined the gun. "Bird shot won't usually kill a man, but at close range it'll definitely rearrange his face."

Mary Lou, Fargo noticed, had reappeared with her basket on her arm.

"I still aim to pick some berries," she informed Fargo. "Is it safe if I stay on our land?"

Fargo considered. It was only midafternon, and he expected no trouble until after dark. Besides, Jesse was topside keeping watch. On the other hand, what woman was "safe" around here after what happened to Holly Nearhood?

"I'll go with you," he decided. Mary Lou beamed, Cranky Man snorted, and Baylor grinned slyly as he went back outside to dig more trip holes.

10

Holding his rein-callused hand in her satin smooth palm, Mary Lou led Fargo along a narrow path deep into the cool woods behind the fields. He kept his eyes shifting to all sides, vigilant for any bird movement or cries that might denote a hidden intruder.

"Won't be long, Mr. Buckskins," she promised, her breath airy with anticipation. "I been *dreamin'* 'bout that peeder a yourn inside me. I like bein' filled up, Skye."

By now Fargo's arousal forced him to limp. "Hush that talk," he admonished. "I'm tryin' to watch for trouble."

She giggled, russet curls bouncing when she leaped over a fallen log. "*Big* log, ain't it?" she teased him, being deliberately ambiguous. "Big, hard log—biggest I ever did see, laws!"

Fargo tried to ignore the saucy temptress, eyes sweeping the thick woods. He wished the Ovaro was along—the stallion was an excellent sentry. Fargo had no hard clues, but now and then the fine hairs on his arms stiffened, as if his body sensed something his mind had yet to perceive.

"Ain't far now, Skye," she promised, leading him across a dry streambed littered with boulders. "Long shanks, I'm gonna climb all over you."

By now her wanton talk had Fargo hotter than a branding iron. Mary Lou reached her destination, a grassy clearing inside a willow thicket.

"Girl," Fargo said, grounding his Henry and sweeping her off her feet to lay her in the soft carpet of grass, "you been tossin' black powder into the fire since we left. It's past talk now."

He didn't bother with her side-lacing shoes, merely yanked her pantaloons down around her slim, well-turned ankles and pushed her dress and chemise up over her hips. This exposed a strawberry-colored bush as soft as pure French wool.

"Looky here," she egged him on, spreading wide her creamy white thighs to expose her coral grotto in the bright sunshine. She glistened with desire, radiating the damp-earth odor of female arousal. Fargo, fingers shaky from lust, fumbled open his fly to release his straining manhood. A quick flex of his buttocks, and he drove his entire length into her slippery-hot sheath, making her cry out with surprised joy.

His hot little Arkansas firecracker started popping off climaxes almost immediately. Each orgasm was like fuel on fuel to the one following, making her cry out louder and louder, thrash harder and harder as Fargo expertly rubbed his curving length across her swollen, pearly nubbin like a bow across a violin.

"Oh, lordy, Skye! *What* are you doing down there? Oh,

oh! My stars, Skye, it's buildin' up . . . it's . . . oh, *oh*! Don't stop, don't you *dare* stop, deeper, long shanks, *deeper*!"

Mary Lou exploded like a steamship boiler as her climax racked her heaving body. Fargo, holding back only from sheer willpower, now felt the floodgates burst open. With a half-dozen powerful, conclusive thrusts he spent himself inside her.

Fargo, for reasons of survival, was not the type to roll off a woman and go to sleep. Nonetheless, doing the mazy waltz with an intense gal like Mary Lou Tutt left him in a mindless trance of pleasure for uncounted minutes, oblivious.

"Skye?"

"Hmm?" His eyelids slowly eased open. Something felt off-kilter, but he couldn't shape the feeling into words.

"How do you find the courage to travel so far? Seems like I been dreamin' forever about somehow movin' out west. I hate it here in Arkansas. Not the land, just all these murdering intruders."

Fargo listened closely to the forest noises, trying to identify what was wrong.

"What's stopping you from going out west?" he asked her. "Your feet bolted to the ground?"

Still lying entwined with Fargo, she waved a hand vaguely to the west. "I tried once and turned around. Too dang much flat dirt to cross. Lookin' at them plains flat-out scairt me. I never seen so much of nothin', just earth and sky."

Damn it, Fargo, what's wrong? the Trailsman demanded of himself. *What is it that's different from when you got here?*

"If you're born on the plains," he assured her, "it's easy to get used to. But they play hell on greenhorns, 'specially women."

Just then Fargo realized what was wrong: the rhythmic insect noise had fallen silent.

"Damn!" Fargo instantly sat up, senses alert.

"Yahh!"

He tensed at the aggressive, masculine battle shout. Before Fargo could even scoop up the Henry, gunshots erupted. Mary Lou screamed as bullets started chunking in all around them.

Cursing, for he could see no one, Fargo rolled on top of Mary Lou to protect her. He felt the wind-rip from several bullets, and heard several more *zwip* through the surrounding grass. When he heard hooves pounding close, however, he rocked up onto his heels and skinned his Colt.

A coal black stallion broke out from the screening timber, bearing straight toward them. Fargo glimpsed hair black as licorice on a hatless head, a pair of Colt Navies in rawhide holsters. Clay Evans bore down on them like the Apocalypse, rapidly levering a Smith & Wesson repeating rifle. His hate-filled eyes were intent on killing both Fargo and Mary Lou.

There was no time to grab the Henry, or even to fire rapidly enough with the single-action Colt by cocking it normally after each shot. Fargo had no choice but to hold the trigger back and fan the hammer rapidly, throwing off his aim. It was a foolish, nickel-novel trick rarely done by an expert shootist. At least, however, he was thus able to toss six rapid shots at their attacker, close enough to tickle his hide and scare him away into the woods.

Always getting caught with your pants down, Fargo, the Trailsman chastised himself as he examined a quaking Mary Lou for injuries.

"Clay Evans, that son of a bitch!" she fumed. "Did he follow us here?"

Fargo shook his head as he helped her to her feet. "Not likely. But I'll tell you why he's here—most likely, he's scouting conditions for tonight's attack. They're makin' a heap of doin's over it."

"You're pretty sure it'll come tonight?"

"Seems likely. That's why they're called night riders. After all, Sheriff Maitland has had plenty of time to 'talk' to Baylor by now and he hasn't."

"Can we whip them, Skye?" she asked as she fell in step with him.

"Whip them? Not hardly. But we *will* stop them."

Mary Lou's fair brow wrinkled in a frown. "With a few more Skye Fargos, sure we could. But there's hundreds of Pukes in this area. I got me a God fear we're all gonna be slaughtered."

The sun was westering by the time Fargo and Mary Lou returned to the house. Cranky Man and his New Haven repeater had replaced Jesse atop the house.

"Ain't no berries in that basket," he called down from the roof when they were close enough.

"Lost 'em in the gun battle," Fargo lied.

Cranky Man loosed a bray of laughter. "Yeah, I heard that. Well, you forgot to 'lose' all the grass stains on your knees and elbows."

"You ain't shaming me, Cranky Man," Mary Lou boldly called up to the Choctaw. "I ain't hitched, and I like bein' pleasured."

"You won't know real pleasure," he assured her, "until you go red."

Fargo laughed. "That's all lip deep."

He made a quick check of his Ovaro and Cranky Man's skewbald. Both horses grazed peacefully in the back pasture. To play it safe, he moved them to the very rear of the fenced property and put them on a short ground tether. In the dark, raiders wouldn't likely spot them back there.

Fargo and Mary Lou next checked the yard surrounding the house. Baylor had done an excellent job of destabilizing the ground with hundreds of trip holes.

"Did Baylor go inside?" Fargo called up to Cranky Man, who was using the brick chimney as a sunbreak.

The Choctaw laughed and pointed north down the dirt road that fronted the house. "Go take a look. *That* boy is slick as an Indian agent."

Fargo and Mary Lou walked out front and immediately spotted Baylor. A small creek paralleled the road, and Baylor had used a mule hitched to a harrow to dig a trench between the creek and a nearby road. Even now water poured over the road, churning it to mud.

"Got the idea while I was digging holes," the oldest Tutt boy greeted them. "Everybody knows that one good rain around here turns the roads into hog wallows. I done it on the other side of the house, too. All the trees keep this road pitch black at night. If they hit this mud goin' full bore, it'll knock the vinegar out of 'em."

Fargo grinned, liking it. "Won't stop 'em, but it might

do plenty to dampen their war fever. These bullyboys are used to a free hand and easy battles. Tonight, by God, they'll discover some hard-cash facts."

"This road ain't much used," Baylor added. " 'Specially at night. Tomorrow I'll fill in the trenches, and the road'll dry out quick."

Fargo and Mary Lou went inside the house. Jesse Tutt had been hard at work, dragging furniture in front of the windows to form makeshift breastworks.

"I kallate Ma and the kids," he greeted Fargo, "will be safest in the pantry. No windows, and any stray bullets oughter miss them. Mary Lou will be under the dinner table running the ammo pile."

Fargo nodded. "Good plan. At the first sign of trouble," he told Ma Tutt, "gather up the tads and take cover. Don't leave the house unless they manage to get a serious fire burning."

Near sunset Baylor returned, his shirt plastered to his back with sweat. Cranky Man followed him inside, his usually grumpy features now tight with worry. "You called it, Fargo," he admitted. "Those white devils are coming. I saw a bunch of Pukes gathering on that big hill where we think Devil's Mouth is hid. Lead *will* fly."

"Lead'll fly both ways," Fargo reminded him. "We'll give as good as we get."

Ma Tutt served a quick cold supper of ham sandwiches and apple pie. Afterward, Cranky Man took out his clay pipe and pouch of kinnikinnick, a mixture of white man's tobacco and the dried inner bark of the red willow. Fargo liked the sweet smell of it, and outdoors it kept mosquitoes off.

"I been thinkin'," Cranky Man told Fargo, smoke wreathing his head. "I think I should *stay* on top the house. Them Pukes will have enough lead comin' at 'em from inside the house, they won't likely look up to the roof. Even if they do, that chimney is thick, and besides, it's a bad angle of fire from the ground. I'll see 'em better from up there."

Fargo thought about it, then nodded. "All right, but don't skyline yourself. Keep a low profile."

Just then Joshua Tutt, muttering to himself, returned from a long visit to the four-holer out back. A copy of an old Springfield, Missouri, newspaper was tucked under his arm. He seemed confused by all the heavily armed men in his parlor. His rheumy eyes fixed on the Trailsman and he shook the newspaper for emphasis. "Mr. Fargold, did you know that Tamsen Donner sewed ten-thousand dollars in a quilt she took west? Why, a body could live almost a lifetime on that!"

"Couldn't buy her a cold biscuit up in the Sierra," Fargo said. "Nor even bury the dead, seein's they ate 'em."

"Well, newspapers lie like rugs," Joshua harrumphed. "The damn fools claim Donner Summit ain't the only time folks ate each other out west."

"That's no lie," Fargo gainsaid. "I myself once trailed with an explorer named Bill Williams who freely admitted he once ate a trail companion in starving times."

Mary Lou turned white as new linen. "And you stayed around after knowing that?"

Fargo grinned. "Well, let's just say I never walked ahead of him on the trail."

Mary Lou slapped his arm. "You're lying!"

"Maybe. Maybe not."

"Well, human suffering," she chastised him, "is no joking matter. Them poor Donners."

Fargo let it go, knowing more important matters were at hand. But he had heard too damn much during his life about "human suffering," when the cold truth was that most of it was unnecessary, simply caused by mule-headed stupidity, especially out west. Shoddy trail discipline, foolish decisions, inexcusable ignorance, hair-trigger tempers, suicidal panic, carelessly stored food—these led to most hardships, not tragic fate or evil Indians.

Just then a chorus of loud curses and horses neighing reached Fargo's ears from the road out front.

"Here's the fandango!" he called out, levering a round into the Henry's chamber. "They've hit the mud trap. Douse all the lights but a candle. Ammo pile, gents!"

Experience had taught Fargo how the ammo pile was important in a scrape against a superior force. Baylor, Jesse, Fargo, and a suddenly purposeful Joshua Tutt threw, all of their ammunition into a pile under the table. Mary Lou, long familiar with various firearms, had insisted on reloading weapons while each man switched to his backup firearm. Timed well, it avoided the dangerous pauses needed to reload.

"What the *hell*?" Fargo demanded, watching Cranky Man. Before he went back onto the roof, the Choctaw paused to tie a heavy leather abdominal cuirass, or flexible armor, around his midsection.

"Took it off a dead bluecoat out in the Nations," Cranky Man explained. "They're uncomfortable as all hell, but soldiers know Indians always aim for the belly—it's a big target and leads to a slow, hard death like fire in your gut. This will stop most arrows and some bullets."

"Maybe so, but it didn't save the soldier you took it off of. Just be careful up on that roof, you old grifter," Fargo said as his friend headed outside. "These killers tonight will aim for your muzzle flash, not your gut. Move after every shot."

Mary Lou crawled under the table, scared but determined. Acting like it was just larks, Ma Tutt herded the kids into the pantry while Joshua Tutt took up a window position with his long .54 Jennings rifle, pulling the mule-ear hammer to full cock. Jesse, Baylor, and Fargo took up positions so that all four sides of the house were covered.

Fargo heard bit rings rattling as the first riders cleared the mud and approached the house.

"Send out Baylor!" a voice commanded, "and the rest of you live!"

"That's Jimbo Powers, leader of the local Pukes," Jesse called over to Fargo. "I know his voice."

"Clear out now, Powers," Fargo roared back in a voice powerful enough to fill a canyon, "and *you* will live to see another sunrise! I don't turn men over to Judge Lynch."

"You had your chance, you abolitionist trash! Now you'll reap the whirlwind! Put at 'em, boys!"

By now more riders surrounded the house. Fargo wanted them in motion as soon as possible because running horses would be more vulnerable to trip holes. So he opened fire first, shoving the Henry's muzzle through a parlor window and firing at the shadowy figures in the moonlight. He made no distinction between horse and rider, not with the lives of innocent women and children on the line.

Surprised grunts and cries of pain greeted his opening

volley. Fargo had plenty of boxes of shells in reserve and emptied the Henry's sixteen-round magazine in an almost continuous burst of fire. As he'd hoped, he forced the night riders into defensive motion before they could return fire.

However, that return fire came with a withering vengeance.

Almost every window in the house shattered at once, and Fargo and the others were forced to duck the exploding glass. Plaster dust filled the house as scores of bullets pockmarked the walls. Glass-framed pictures shattered, lamp shades were shredded, wooden chairs danced as rounds rocked them every which way. Several slugs grazed so close that Fargo felt them tickle his hair and beard.

"Comin' at you, Mary Lou," he shouted, sliding the empty Henry across the floor to her central position under the dining room table.

The only mechanical drawback to the Henry was its difficult-to-load tube magazine. While Mary Lou's adept but trembling fingers took on the task, Fargo jerked his Colt and, more selective this time, emptied it at the Border Ruffians. There was enough moonlight to reveal their plumed hats.

Both animal and human cries, as well as the audible snap of bones, told Fargo the trip holes were having a devastating impact on the attackers. So was the combined fire from inside and atop the house. So many downed horses clogged the way that the Pukes were savagely cursing each other.

Jesse's 20-gauge shotgun roared, and a man screamed hideously when his face took the full brunt of the birdshot. He'd live, Fargo figured, but wish he hadn't—no way would his eyes survive that direct hit. It was Joshua Tutt who most surprised Fargo. Most of the time he acted like a featherbrained idiot, maybe, but not once the war cry sounded. His long Jennings barked with deadly effect, nor did the granite-jawed old patriarch flinch once as enemy bullets hornet-swarmed around him.

"We're dropping them pretty fast!" Fargo shouted to his companions. "But that means burning us out is next. Get ready on water detail."

Again Fargo's frontier intuition panned out. Barely a minute after his warning, flaming torches flew through the shot-out windows. Thanks to the pre-positioned water containers, however, no serious damage was done except for scorched rugs.

Still, Fargo was caught completely off guard when a fizzling stick of dynamite sailed over his head, hit the floor, and rolled fast right toward Mary Lou and the ammo pile.

"God-in-whirlwinds!" Fargo could not worry about covering down now. As Mary Lou froze, shocked sick and silly at the sight of lit dynamite, Fargo leaped to his feet and bolted toward her. As he scooped it up, he realized the fuse was down to a fractional inch.

There was no time—not even the space of an eyeblink— to carry it close enough to a window before tossing it back outside. Picking the nearest window, perhaps thirty feet away, he snapped it hard in an overhand throw. The stick barely nicked the wooden window frame before it arced outside into the yard.

The explosive concussion was so close that dirt and grass came slapping into the house. Hideous screams from without proved that a few Pukes, too, got a good dose of their own bad medicine. Between that blast and the unexpectedly effective defense, the Border Ruffians had temporarily had enough.

When the last of them had retreated, Fargo eased open the front door. "Cranky Man? You still among the living?"

"Living? Fargo, you *are* a caution! Boy, I just saved all your white asses. But, Christ, have we got dead and downed horses to deal with."

A quick check showed that, while there was considerable bullet damage to the house, the defenders were unscathed except for a few minor glass cuts. Cranky Man was right— at least a dozen horses were down, several still alive. Hating the task, Fargo shot them.

"They took their dead and wounded men," he reported when he returned to the house. "At first light, you should rig your mules and pile the dead horses out back. We'll have to pitch in and dig a trench to bury 'em."

Fargo decided that a sentry atop the house was a good idea for the rest of the night. Cranky Man had done his stint, so Fargo, Jesse, and Baylor took turnabout, Fargo standing the first shift.

"You know where my bedroom is, long shanks," Mary Lou whispered as he headed out into the darkness. "The window's shattered now, so you won't even have to come through the house. I'll be waitin'."

11

Despite the strong temptation, Fargo's tryst with Mary Lou never happened. Knowing how these terror gangs liked to use follow-up attacks, he had no plans to get caught yet again with his pants down. At first light the men began the unpleasant task of collecting and burying horses.

"Place looks like a shooting gallery," Ma Tutt carped as she fired up the cookstove for breakfast. "Laws! Ain't nary a wall what didn't get shot up."

"But we still got Baylor, Ma," Jesse reminded her. "Them Pukes was aiming to swing him from a tree."

The old dame wiped her hands on her apron, watching Fargo from grateful eyes. "That's God's truth, Jesse. We can thank Mr. Fargo for that."

"Mr. Fargold is a credit to his dam, Ma," Joshua Tutt said as he buttoned his suspender loops, his old hickory-nut face sad.

"It's Fargo, not Fargold," she corrected him.

"But he can't work miracles," Joshua continued, ignoring her. "I see now that we *will* be squoze out. That Evans bunch got the Pukes on their side."

"And the violence is spreading fast," Ma Tutt said, using a long-handled toasting fork to brown some bread. "Lands, every drumstick of a boy in these parts wants to get him a rifle and join the sport."

"Far as you folks getting squeezed out," Fargo said as

he pushed up to the breakfast table, "that's cowplop. Sure, the Evanses and the Pukes are all back-scratching each other. Nothing new there."

"The so-called law is in it, too," Baylor reminded their guest. "Hollis Maitland is feedin' at the same trough with the killers and thieves."

Fargo attacked, with gusto, a delicious meal of buckwheat cakes, soda biscuits, and sausage gravy.

"I don't try to buck the law," Fargo replied, reluctantly interrupting his chewing. "Just so it's *honest* law. Don't fret none about Hollis. I think he's scared, not criminal, and he's soon going to come to Jesus."

Mary Lou, wearing a blue anchor print, said, "Oh, botheration! You're a mite sure of yourself, Mr. Buckskins. But after losing the fight last night, they still need a scapegoat for the murder of Holly."

"Had to be Scooter Evans that done it," Baylor fumed. "He's one kill-crazy son of a bitch. I mean to bury a spur in his ass when I catch him, then gut him like a fish on a stump."

Fargo wiped his mouth. "Catch him? Now, just hold your whist, farm boy. They *want* to draw you out so they can toss the net around you. You and Jesse both stay right here to home. The war kettle is on the fire now, and this fight has to play out."

"What about you?" Mary Lou demanded. "You're deserting us now?"

"If you were a man," Fargo replied, "I'd slap you dizzy for that remark."

"If she *was* a man, Fargo," Cranky Man muttered, "you'd have some explaining to do."

Ma Tutt sent a searing glance at Fargo, which he avoided.

"Anyway," he told Mary Lou, "I never quit a fight until it's over. But we can't conquer the world from your parlor. Me and Cranky Man will be riding out in a few minutes to locate Devil's Mouth."

Cranky Man, dressed in sturdy trousers of bleached canvas and his best leather shirt adorned with beadwork, sent a quick, surprised glance at Fargo. He hummed the Funeral March to make his point.

"Another thing," Fargo told Mary Lou. "I *can't* stay here now or your house will become a target range. From here on out I patrol the area, showing myself plenty. When I'm not looking for Devil's Mouth or scouting, I'll hole up in Cranky Man's cave close to Lead Hill."

"Now that the truce is over," Jesse worried aloud, "what's to keep them snakebit skunks from hittin' our house any damn time they please?"

"Sauce for the goose," Fargo replied.

Jesse frowned. "Huh?"

"We hit the Evans house," Fargo clarified. "Tonight, if possible, sooner the better. Turnabout is fair play, so we'll see how they like it. We ain't got the firepower they mustered, but we'll have total surprise on our side."

"Kill one fly, kill a million," old Joshua belted out. His shaggy white eyebrows arched and his mouth set itself hard. He was so mad his bones seemed to stand out and his eyes to sink in. "A mighty fortress is our God! By eternal thunder, *I'll* be riding with you young fellas tonight."

Everyone except Fargo and Cranky Man started to protest. Fargo knew every family tree had its nuts, but as last night proved, Joshua was clearheaded when danger threatened. He fought bravely and coolly even as bullets swarmed past his head.

"Be honored to have you, sir," Fargo told the patriarch, quelling all protests.

Fargo had already checked on the Ovaro and Cranky Man's skewbald, finding both horses safe in the back pasture. The two men quickly washed out back in soft cistern water. While they tacked their mounts for the trail, Fargo kept a wary eye out.

"Too damn many timbered sidehills around here," he complained as he cinched the girth. "Ambushers' haven."

"I'll be fine," Cranky Man bragged, fingering the magic pebbles around his neck.

"That's right, those turn bullets into sand," Fargo remembered. "And you believe that?"

"Sure's hell do. Indian medicine is more powerful than white man's."

Quicker than thought Fargo's Colt was drawn, cocked, and kissing the Choctaw's temple. "Say when, and I'll tweak the trigger."

Cranky Man went pale. "Leather that gun, weed face.

I ain't *sure* them pebbles work. Could be fakes made by white men."

"I had no plans to shoot," Fargo assured him. "And I ain't mockin' your medicine. Just reminding you not to get cocky with the magic stuff."

Fargo stepped into the stirrup and pushed up and over. He and Cranky Man were just passing the kitchen door when Joshua Tutt struggled outside with a butter churn. When Fargo had left the house, Ma Tutt had been moving the dasher up and down to bring butter.

"You two takin' the buckboard to town?" Joshua called out.

Cranky Man and Fargo exchanged a quick look. Brain-addled Joshua had already forgotten their plans.

"Not this trip, sir," Fargo replied.

"That's a pity. We usually put the cream in the buck-board when we leave for town," Joshua explained. "The roads is so cussed bad all the joltin' churns the cream into butter by the time we get back."

"That old man's only got one oar in the water," Cranky Man remarked quietly as the two men rode out. "But I like him."

Fargo nodded. "Damn shame, his bein' head-kicked. Hell, I don't care about him calling me Mr. Fargold. But his family could use his leadership. These are dangerous times."

"Not for me until you showed up."

"We ain't joined at the hip," Fargo said, his lake-water eyes in constant motion. "Go break into more houses, I won't stop you."

"Nah, I mean to stick. You're a rare thing in these parts, Fargo—a man who thinks honor and courage trump the profit motive."

" 'Preciate that," Fargo said sincerely. "But I *don't* walk on water, remember that. We could both end up sucking wind through a dozen bullet holes."

They were still on the Tutt's rich bottomland, and well-tasseled corn rippled in the breeze. Soon, Fargo thought, it would leaf and come to the full ear—assuming it wasn't destroyed. For a spell both men fell silent, for now they were approaching the large hill, on Evans property, where they suspected the cave called Devil's Mouth was hidden.

A peddler's wagon rattled past, and a cautious Fargo palmed the butt of his Colt.

By the time the sun had been up for an hour, the day had turned tissue fine. Bird chatter reassured Fargo that no large groups of Border Ruffians were lurking on or near the hill. However, a sentry or two could be hidden up there.

Cranky Man started another loud complaint, but Fargo waved him quiet. "For an Indian you talk too damn much. Say little and miss nothing."

Using a skill Fargo had perfected on the open plains, he sent his hearing out beyond the immediate surroundings.

"Seems safe," he told Cranky Man in a whisper. "But I got a gut hunch we best get ready for a set-to."

The two riders reined off the trail and let their horses walk up the wooded slope. Fargo had his Colt in hand; the repeating rifle Cranky Man had claimed from a dead Puke protruded from his saddle scabbard.

"Any trouble will come from there," Fargo remarked quietly, pointing toward a hogback, a ridge with a sharp crest and abruptly sloping sides. They dotted the Arkansas landscape.

"This is like robbing a bird's nest on the ground," Cranky Man scoffed. "Last night's attack has got you nerve-rattled, Fargo."

The Trailsman had to agree that was possible. The birds were still chattering away, and the trusty Ovaro was calmly nibbling at pine needles carpeting the hillside. Golden fingers of light poked through the trees, adding beauty to the peace and quiet.

However, the tree cover stopped about twenty feet ahead, giving way to a broad expanse dotted with bluebonnets and daisies dying in the long drought. Even the normally hearty fox grapes and wild mint looked shriveled. Fargo hadn't seen such withered vegetation since he'd ridden through the parched hills of San Diego's Mission Valley.

He thumb-cocked his short iron and pressured his stallion with both knees. "Open ground ahead," he told Cranky Man. "Skin that rifle—it's no use to us in the boot."

"Fargo, you got the balls of a stud bull," the Choctaw roweled him. "But you worry like a schoolgirl. The worst thing hidden on that hogback is a mad dog."

"I said get that rifle up," Fargo snapped, and this time Cranky Man obeyed.

As they edged out from cool shadows to hot sunshine, Fargo got a good view of a hilltop clearing carved out by lightning. The yellow-brown grass was clearly trampled by many hooves—was, in fact, barely growing in places.

Fargo wiped sweat off his forehead with the back of his wrist. "We're close to Devil's Mouth," he muttered. "Look at that clearing."

"Yeah, strange place to corral horses," Cranky Man agreed.

"I'm thinking the cave entrance is on the back side of the hill," Fargo said. "The hoofprints head that way."

They were halfway across the open expanse of bluebonnets and daisies, and Fargo felt ice replace his blood when the Ovaro suddenly lifted his head, nose sampling the air.

"Shit!" he swore, reaching across to punch Cranky Man's shoulder. "Get set to buck the tiger!"

Fargo's voice had barely fallen silent before a hidden rifle barked and a bullet scraped his saddle fender. At least two shooters opened up, and in the bright sunlight muzzle flash got lost. Finally, though, Fargo noticed wisps of blue smoke curling up from the hogback.

"There!" he shouted to Cranky Man above the hammering racket of gunfire. "We'll never overrun 'em across this open ground. They'll drop our horses quicker 'n scat. Best we can do is toss a wall of lead at 'em, drive 'em to cover while we get out of the weather."

Even before Fargo finished speaking, Cranky Man's saddle horn caught a slug and broke off, smacking the Choctaw on the jaw with the force of a fist. Fargo fought to keep the Ovaro from turning sideways, knowing the stallion would then be an easy target. The Trailsman drew on reserves of courage and willed himself steady. He holstered his Colt, snatched the Henry from its saddle sheath and levered a round into the chamber.

Under withering fire, both riders forged up the slope a few more yards to unnerve the ambushers. Fargo sent lead whistling and hissing with a vengeance, and Cranky Man's repeating rifle chimed in. Up on the sharp crest of the hogback, geysers of rock dust filled the air as their bullets took effect. For a moment, two men could be seen retreating down the back slope.

"Clay Evans and his crazy cousin Scooter!" Cranky Man explained as he and Fargo whirled their mounts to escape. "Too bad they got the high ground."

"They'll end up with just six feet of *low* ground when this plays out," Fargo vowed, now riding in the safety of the trees. "But we got another problem: all the shooting musta warned the Pukes—hear that?"

Cranky Man nodded. "Riders headed this way like bats outta hell."

"Lots of riders," Fargo qualified. "We won't shoot our way out, so get set to turn that skewbald into an express pony."

By the time the two riders reached the trail again, the Border Ruffians in their plumed hats and butternut clothing were nearly in rifle range, approaching hard from the south. About a dozen, Fargo estimated, sending up a cloud of boiling yellow dust.

" 'Me and Cranky Man will be riding out in a few minutes to locate Devil's Mouth,' " the Choctaw said sarcastically, quoting Fargo from earlier.

"I think we *did* locate it, or mighty near," Fargo replied, slapping the reins across the Ovaro's flanks.

"A-huh, and damn near got me shot into the deal. I'll be damn lucky if I don't slide forward off this ruined saddle."

"We'll replace it," Fargo shouted back. "Far as getting shot—you got magic pebbles, remember? Bullets into sand."

"We'll soon find out," Cranky Man said. "Here comes the Kentucky pills."

The pursuing Pukes had indeed opened up. Most of their shots were out of range although now and then a round passed so close Fargo felt the wind flutter.

"Nix on that," Fargo shouted when Cranky Man reached back for his New Haven Arms rifle. "Firing to the rear will slow you down. For now let's try to outrun the bastards."

At first Fargo's plan worked well. The Ovaro, who had once won a grueling, daylong horse race in the vicious Salt Desert of Utah Territory, stretched out his long neck and lengthened his powerful stride. For some time Cranky Man's horse kept pace, and the pursuers were hard-pressed to keep them in sight.

Then . . . disaster. Cranky Man's mount, unshod like most Indian ponies, stepped down hard on a sharp rock, bruising a hoof and pulling up lame.

"Don't stop, Fargo," the half blood said, turning pale. "It's the dirt nap for me, but you can still save your ass."

"That's a hell of a thing to say to me," Fargo protested as he wheeled the Ovaro around. "Damned ignorant savage."

Fargo had never left a man in the lurch and would rather die than start now—especially since Cranky Man had saved the Trailsman's life with some fancy knife work.

"Well, when fleeing ceases to be an option," Fargo said, "then it's time to attack."

He whipped the Ovaro up to a gallop and headed straight for the surprised pursuers.

His Henry was still empty from the hilltop scrape, and too cumbersome to load on the gallop. So he shucked out his Colt and, screaming like a madman, sent six bullets into the pursuing pack. A horse went down, tripping several more. Fargo didn't leave it there—he swung open the Colt's loading gate and thumbed in reloads.

Meantime, the enraged Border Ruffians were turning the air deadly with so many rounds Fargo's vision went blurry. He placed his fear outside of himself and dropped the Colt's notch sight on the apparent leader of this patrol.

The distance, and the Ovaro's rapid motion, made this a tough shot for a handgun. Fargo's first two slugs got nothing but air. Number three, however, kissed the mistress. His slug punched into the man's forehead, and ropes of blood spurted from his nose and ears. His eyes lost their focus and turned to glass as the body toppled from the saddle like a sack of grain.

However, Fargo knew he couldn't let up despite the slugs whiffing past him. With his three remaining bullets he managed to drop a horse and wipe another man out of the saddle. By now, with their leader and another comrade killed, and nearly half the horses entangled on the trail, the Pukes had lost their bravado. Playing a hunch, Fargo jerked his unloaded Henry from its boot and held it up long enough for the Border Ruffians to recognize the brass frame reflecting in the sunlight: a sixteen-shot Henry repeater!

They had no way of knowing it wasn't loaded, and none

of them hung around to find out. As soon as the horse pileup was untangled, the surviving attackers turned tail and fled.

Fargo finally drew rein, relief flooding through him.

"A bluff is a fine thing when it works," he remarked quietly to the Ovaro. "Damn good thing they didn't call my hand."

The stallion had been running hard in punishing heat, so Fargo walked him back toward Cranky Man to cool him out.

"Fargo," Cranky Man greeted him, "I thank you all to hell. I was singing my death song when you attacked them Pukes. Maybe you don't walk on water, but you *can* work miracles. And that stallion of yours moves along like Going was his ma's name and Fast his pa's."

Fargo grinned through his mask of dust. "Yep. He gets most of the credit, as usual. But let's not be reciting our coups just yet. Nothing's really changed. This area's lousy with Pukes, and they still got an ally in the Evans clan."

Cranky Man nodded. "All champing at the bit to free your soul. And I'm here to tell you, a man gets tired of looking over his shoulder."

"True enough. But it ain't just me. They mean to rub out the entire Tutt family—and Clay Evans has got 'special' plans for Mary Lou. With Pukes pouring over the border from Missouri, plenty more innocent people in Arkansas will be doing the hurt dance."

"Straight arrow. But we just found out the cave is now guarded."

Fargo was silent at the reminder. The problem of that damned hidden cave seemed like a mountain in his path.

"Guarded or not," he finally replied, "Devil's Mouth is the key to everything. We'll leave it alone for now—we've got tonight's visit to the Evans house. But come hell or high water, we're gonna locate that cave, and then we're gonna clean it out."

12

Cranky Man's skewbald was not seriously lamed, just suffering a minor bruise that required massaging and a few hours of rest. Since the Choctaw's cave was only a mile away, just north of Lead Hill, both men led their horses by the bridle reins.

"Oh, hell," Fargo muttered, "here comes Lead Hill's jackleg sheriff. Wonder what he means to arrest me for now."

Hollis Maitland, looking even older than his fifty years, drew closer on a big gray gelding.

"Heard the shooting," he greeted them, casting a puzzled glance at Cranky Man. "Pukes?"

Fargo ignored the question. "Were you part of the raid last night on the Tutt farm?"

"My hand to God," Maitland replied, "I've *never* taken an active hand in the crimes hatched by the Evanses."

"I'll believe that much," Fargo granted. "You don't seem to have the black heart of a full criminal. But you told me you intended to *question* Baylor, and you never did it."

Maitland, perhaps feeling awkward looking down upon the unmounted men, swung down himself. "No, I didn't," he admitted. "See, at first I really thought Baylor mighta done it. Then, when I conned it over some, I knew it had to be Scooter Evans. The crime's got his sick mind stamped all over it."

"You're saying you had no foreknowledge of the crime?"

The sheriff's seamed face twitched. "I was told that a 'terrible crime' was coming up, yeah, and that I was s'posed to arrest Baylor for it. But that's all I knew, I swear."

"That's *all*?" Fargo retorted sarcastically. "Damn brilliant detective work, Maitland. You know, a man who holds a candle for the devil does the devil's work."

Maitland's jowly face looked so ashamed that Fargo almost regretted the rebuke.

"The devil's work," Maitland repeated. "You nailed it, Fargo. That's why I'm here right now, looking for you. Langston Evans has already promised me that Scooter will kill me—and kill me hard—if I don't nail my colors to their mast. But I don't care anymore, not after what was done to poor Holly. I'm done being scared into silence."

Fargo studied the lawman's contrite face and decided to believe him.

"All right, Maitland, you were scared for your life. That's understandable—you're only one man in a sea of killers. And you say you've avoided taking an active part in any crimes. But I'll warn you now: the U.S. Army *will* be coming into this soon. Anything you tell me now about this Tutt-Evans feud will help your case."

"Feud, my ass," the sheriff replied. "Langston Evans' hawg-stupid brother Daniel killed himself cleaning his rifle. So Langston promptly killed a Tutt in so-called revenge for the supposed murder."

Fargo didn't look a bit surprised. "So that's the way of it. Like I suspected from the get-go, it's all about getting that fine piece of bottomland in their hands for when the Homestead Act passes, which could happen any day now."

Maitland nodded. "The Tutt farm is one of the finest in Arkansas. But there's more trouble on the spit, Fargo. Bad trouble meant to make the Pukes rich and leave Jesse Tutt dancing on air. You know what a bullion coach is?"

"Hauls newly minted gold and silver coins to major banks."

Maitland loosed a troubled sigh. "Yup. And later today there'll be a bullion coach heading from the temporary mint in Kansas City to the banks in Little Rock. A bunch of Pukes, led by Jimbo Powers, plan to hit it—a complete rubout—and blame it on Jayhawkers led by Jesse."

"Bullion coaches are well guarded," Fargo pointed out. "As many as ten well-armed soldiers."

"Powers can easy muster a hunnert riders, none of 'em chicken guts."

Fargo had to concede the point. Whatever their many faults, the Border Ruffians lived up to their name. "Where," he asked, "will the coach actually cross Arkansas? Near here?"

Maitland shook his head. "It'll come straight south from Kansas City, entering the state west of here. The strike is planned for West Fork, an empty region just north of the Boston Mountains."

Fargo cursed. "Obviously they're on the road by now. Have you telegraphed anybody?"

Maitland shrugged helplessly. "We have lines strung, but the railroad picked Bull Shoals for their nearest station."

Fargo took his point: no railroad, no telegraph station. Not in a place as remote as Lead Hill—a mere pimple on Nowhere's ass.

"I sometimes work for the army," Fargo explained, "and they gave me a pocket relay I carry in a saddle pocket. Are your lines humming?"

Maitland nodded.

"I can shinny up a pole," Fargo said, swinging up into leather, "and splice into the line. I'm a mite clumsy at tapping out Morse, but we can try to warn the garrison at Fort Smith."

"That's about fifty miles south of West Fork," the sheriff said. "Good chance they could get a patrol up there in time."

"Show me the nearest pole," Fargo ordered, pulling the small pocket relay out to examine its various parts. "And then I strongly recommend that you fade until this is over, Maitland. I've seen Scooter Evans' handiwork, and they're going to suspect you ratted them out."

Maitland stubbornly shook his head. "I already pissed them off by not arresting Baylor, so why stop now? I was elected sheriff of Lead Hill and it's about damn time I measured up to men like you, Fargo, or at least *try* to. I been scared so long I forgot there's a set between my legs. Better to buck out in smoke than live your life running scared."

Fargo had not forgotten Maitland's many sins. However, the Trailsman also believed in redemption through honor and courage. He feared for the aging lawman's safety here in Lead Hill, but applauded his decision to stand up like a man with gumption.

"I'd be proud to have you on our side, Hollis," Fargo told him as Cranky Man, too, stepped up into leather. Maitland beamed with pride, and then cast a suspicious glance at Cranky Man.

"Say, John, ain't you s'posed to be out west in the Nations?"

Cranky Man met the lawman's eyes. "And ain't *you* s'posed to report it when you learn about crimes being hatched? Why start playing honest star man with me? *I* been fighting the enemy you've been helping."

Maitland flushed beet red. "Damn! I don't cotton to sass from an Indian, but your English is as clear as your logic. Sorry I asked."

"Both you jays pipe down," Fargo ordered. "Hollis Maitland, meet Cranky Man. Now let's get a wiggle on—we got a message to send before heaven gets packed with fresh souls."

The evening of Fargo's third day in the dangerous northwest Arkansas region produced an ivory moon as big as a dinner plate. Ruddy lamplight glowed in the parlor windows of the sprawling Evans house, but the gathering within was hardly festive. The Big Boss was fit to be tied.

"Button your ears back, alla you, 'cause I'm only going to say this once," Langston Evans told the assemblage, his face splotched with anger. "I *warned* you this buttinsky bastard Fargo is hell on two sticks. I've had my belly full of all the goddamn excuses, he should've died ten times by now."

The group included Langston's boys Clay and Dobie, their cousin Scooter, and Jimbo Powers, plumed hat resting on one knee. Hollis Maitland, with Fargo's blessing, had also shown up—not doing so would have convicted him for the aborted robbery, earlier that day, of the bullion coach near West Fork. Also present was the hatchet-faced Matilda "Maw-maw" Evans, who was calmly rocking as she knit a shawl.

"But, Pa," Dobie protested, "ain't no proof a-tall Fargo called in them soldiers. Hell's bells, it coulda been Hollis here who done it."

Langston, who was pacing the room like a caged lion, paused to stare at the sheriff from eyes like glowing coals. "I pondered on that possibility. What say, Hollis? You a secret crusader?"

"Crusader?" Maw-maw laughed so hard she dropped a stitch.

"Check with Bob Knowles, the telegrapher at Bull Shoals," Maitland protested. "By law every telegram is logged. Last one I sent was two months ago, to my sister in Illinois."

All this was true. It was Fargo who sent the emergency message to Fort Smith, and because he spliced into the line with a relay, the telegram wasn't logged at this end—only at Fort Smith.

"I believe you, Hollis, but only because you ain't got the balls to be a crusader like Fargo," the Evans patriarch decided, a sneer in his tone. "But don't *ever* try to slicker me—I'm smarter than you look. Scooter, what happens to this old compost heap if he ever sticks it to us again like he did by refusing to arrest Baylor?"

Scooter's mud-colored eyes cut to Hollis. He watched the lawman from his sullen deadpan. He was built like a granite block and looked strong as horseradish. Forming a pair of scissors with two fingers, he said, "Snip snip. From a stallion to a gelding."

Hollis paled, knowing full well the crazy bastard was being literal. The sheriff would be dead already, but the Big Boss decided to believe his lie about how Baylor overpowered him during an attempted arrest.

"I ain't tryin' to slicker anybody," he assured Langston.

"Hell," Maw-maw cut in, her hard mouth curling into a sneer, "*look* at Hollis. The fool don't know whether to shit or go blind. Cut off his balls? What balls? I bet he has to squat to piss. Scooter done *his* part with Holly Nearhood, but our 'sheriff' here didn't—the point was to arrest Baylor Tutt, not let him put a dress on you."

Maitland's face twisted, but he said nothing.

"Maw-maw's right as rain," her husband chimed in. "And, Hollis, what about your damned display of 'courage' in the Three Sisters? Fargo sent one of Jimbo's boys to eternity, giving you a perfect excuse to arrest that meddling bastard."

"You can't arrest a man like Skye Fargo for trumped-up crimes," Hollis objected. "He's all grit and a yard wide. That killing in the Sisters was self-defense, and the bartender swore to it. Christ, Fargo whipped your boy Clay, cowed a saloon full of well-armed men, and fought off dozens of night riders at the Tutt place."

Langston's face flushed beet red with anger, the color even more enhanced by his thick white mane of hair. "Shit take it, Hollis! I don't care if the lanky son of a bitch can kill a cougar with a shoe. You'll have *one* more chance, law dog, to prove you own a pair. Nobody euchres Langston Evans. *No*body."

Clay, his licorice black hair thick with axle grease, had been stewing since Hollis mentioned how Fargo had whipped him. "Fargo ain't nothing but Jayhawker trash. A spy sent down from Kansas."

Langston shook his head in pure frustration. "Don't be a fool *all* your life, boy. Fargo ain't flying no man's flag. He's what you call an eternal outsider—the most dangerous kind of man to tangle with. You should know that by now. He whipped you into the dirt."

"Whipped? That son of a bitch coldcocked me," Clay protested. "It wa'n no proper whipping. And he's bird-dogging my meat."

"Tarnal hell, boy!" Langston exploded. "You're worrying about fleas while tigers eat us alive. Won't be too long now before Fargo sniffs out Jimbo's cave. Matter fact, he got within spitting distance of it today. You know there's dozens of horses kept there and valuable supplies."

"Not to mention," Maw-maw said, still rocking at a slow pace, "that we need to get control of the townsite charter before that new Homestead Act passes. And we ain't gettin' control of one damn thing so long as Fargo is left alive."

"It had to be Fargo," Jimbo Powers spoke up, "who sent word to them soldiers. But *how* did he get word of the planned heist?"

Again all eyes turned to Hollis Maitland.

"If I told Fargo," the sheriff said, "I sure's hell wouldn't be here tonight. In fact, I'd be fifty miles out of town and still riding."

"Your word," Langston snapped, "ain't worth a whorehouse token."

Nonetheless, he waved a dismissive hand toward Hollis and turned to face Powers. "Jimbo, I know *you* can fight. But I'm starting to wonder if these men of yours are all gurgle and no guts. First they let Fargo single-handedly buffalo them at the saloon, even killing one. Then, today, they took off like scalded dogs when a few soldiers showed up."

"A few? Langston, there were at least forty, all armed with the new repeating carbines. And there were already ten messenger riders with the coach, all carrying sawed-off express guns. I only took thirty men."

"Why only thirty?"

"With this drought, I had to keep down the dust puffs."

Langston's face relented somewhat. After all, he had given Powers the tip about the bullion coach as a reward for valuable services rendered over the years. Powers and his men were denied their swag, and who knew how they might react?

"Well, after all, Jimbo, you were snookered along with the rest of us. I apologize for my short temper. But let's face it, there's a mort of work to be done, and it can't *get* done unless we cooperate close in killing Fargo."

Five men held their horses by the bridle reins in the humid darkness, watching the well-lighted Evans house below them in a hollow.

"That big gray tied to the porch rail is Hollis Maitland's horse," Skye Fargo told his companions. "Hollis said he always gets sent away early, so we'll wait till he leaves. I'd prefer to strike while he's there—it gives him more cover. But he doesn't know this attack is coming, and it might drive him away from our side—or even kill him."

Cranky Man and the three Tutt men—Joshua, Baylor, and Jesse—surrounded Fargo in the moonlit darkness. The hum of insects and the snuffling of the horses were the only sounds.

"That sorrel is one of Jim Powers' mounts," Baylor said, his face grim. "He led the attack on our place last night. Just in case we need any proof him and Langston are chummy, there it is, sure as we're standing here."

"Plead guilty and there's no jury," old Joshua interjected. "But they must still face the judge."

His boys sent an apologetic glance toward Fargo, embarrassed by their father's soft-brained remarks. Fargo, however, had noticed how the tough old Appalachian grew more lucid when the fight was on. His remark just now made perfect sense to the Trailsman.

"They're about to face the judge, Mr. Tutt," Fargo assured him, "but *not* the executioner. We're here to shoot up the house, not deliberately kill anyone. If it happens, it happens—by their own choice, lead will be flying thick and furious. But no man here tonight aims to kill except as a last resort."

Cranky Man gave a soft grunt. "Christ, Fargo, why'n't we just powder their butts and tuck 'em in while we're at it?"

"Cranky Man's right," hotheaded Jesse chipped in. "Skye, you're the boss, and I'll follow you into hell carrying an empty rifle. But them slaver sons of bitches didn't worry about killing *us* last night. Onliest thing saved us was being ready."

"Eye for an eye," Joshua approved.

"Old Testament justice suits me," Fargo said. "But there has to be a difference between justice and vengeance. A man who descends to the criminal's level has lost his right to be called decent. And once a man squanders his honor, the hell's he got left?"

The degradation of human nature under adversity— Fargo knew that's what a man had to resist if he was going to survive and win with his self-respect intact. Silence ensued while the men digested his remarks. Baylor, Jesse, finally even Cranky Man, nodded agreement.

Joshua's next comment proved he was crazy like a fox. "Our friend Mr. Fargold has struck a lode, boys. 'If gold will rust, what then will iron do?' "

Cranky Man, who preferred white men's calligraphy to their odd conversations, spoke up impatiently. "Stupid rule, Fargo, us leaving the cheer water behind. Hell, I require a nip now and then to wash my teeth."

"Then you must wash 'em one at a time," Fargo countered, " 'cause you're always nipping. Last thing we need in a shooting fray is a drunk firing at his own men."

"My mood is even more foul," Cranky Man warned him, "when I'm sober."

"There goes Hollis," Baylor cut in suddenly. "Just stepped off the porch."

"We'll wait a spell," Fargo said. "No matter how you slice it, the Evans faction will suspect Maitland of being involved, especially since we're striking after he leaves. But there's no good way around the strike. The quickest way to go under is to let bullyboys know it's easy to kill you."

In silence all five men watched Hollis unwrap the reins and step up into leather, rheumatism slowing his movements. He seemed an almost mournful figure, in the generous moon wash, as he reined his gelding around toward the lonely road to Lead Hill.

The later the better, anyway, so Fargo waited at least a half hour after Maitland left. Then, grabbing the horn and stabbing his boot into a stirrup, he told the rest, "Get horsed. They *will* shoot back and there's a bright moon, so don't pause to reload except in dark places. They'll likely pick the upper floor, so watch every window for muzzle flash."

"Got that hear-nothing charm I gave you?" Cranky Man asked Fargo. "It'll let you sneak up on anybody unheard."

"Yeah, it's in my pocket, but I don't set much store by that hoodoo stuff."

A long, gentle slope lay between them and the east side of the two-story house. Fargo led the way, but Cranky Man quickly rode up alongside him. "You'll see, Fargo. Nobody in that house is going to hear us until we open fire. I gave everybody else a hear-nothing charm, too."

"Keep your voice down, you damn fool," Fargo admonished. "Charm or no charm, we're close to the house."

Behind Fargo, Joshua whispered to his youngest boy, "Jesse, get them reins tight. Your horse jerks his head, you'll buck your aim."

Fargo grinned in the moonlit darkness. The old man hadn't lost his battle sense, at least.

He patted the Ovaro's neck to calm him. At that very moment, Cranky Man's skewbald gave out a loud nicker. Fargo felt his scalp tighten.

"Don't worry," the confident Choctaw assured the others, "those hear-nothing charms will—"

A front door banged open, spilling oily light out into the yard. "Who goes there?" demanded an authoritative voice.

Fargo immediately blasted at the door with his Henry,

and it was slammed shut. There went the crucial element of surprise.

"Big medicine, my ass," Fargo growled at Cranky Man. Then he raised his voice. "You know what to do, men! Stay in motion, reload in the shadows, make it lively for 'em!"

Because they had been forewarned, the men inside the house began firing almost as soon as the attackers did. The lanterns were quickly extinguished, leaving nothing but muzzle flash to mark the defenders' locations. Nonetheless, Fargo's group unleashed an impressive spray of lead and buckshot, soon shattering every window in the house.

However, something troubled Fargo. Counting Jimbo Powers, there should have been at least five guns blazing at them, six if Maw-maw pitched into the game. Only four were firing so far, two downstairs and two up. Even so, the hissing *whiff* of slugs menaced the riders.

Fargo, holding on to the running Ovaro with his knees, emptied the Henry, then booted it and shifted to his Colt. Six more red muzzle streaks stabbed at the darkness as he emptied the single-action revolver.

Fargo needed to find a shadowy pocket where he could reload his weapons. First, though, it was time to fight fire with fire. Two coal-oil soaked torches were stuffed in his saddlebags. Thumb-scratching a lucifer into flame, he ignited one and flung it through a side window. He somehow managed to fling the second torch through an upstairs window. Panicked shouts soon rose from inside the house.

"Good work, hair-face!" Cranky Man shouted as he passed Fargo while rounding a corner of the house, working the lever of his rifle like a pump handle.

Fargo faded back into the shadowy backyard where a rickety wooden jakes was located. Thumbing reloads into the Colt took a matter of moments, but he was slowed down by the Henry's clumsy, slow-loading magazine. He had pressed perhaps eight rounds into the long tube when the door of the jakes swung open with a sound like a cat meowing.

Fargo felt his stomach churn with dread when Scooter Evans emerged into the moonlight, a huge hogleg pistol aimed at Fargo's lights. His rabbit teeth were bared in a sick grin of triumph.

"Man steps outside to take him a shit," Scooter greeted

him, "and the shit comes to him. Throw down that long iron, Fargo, then the short iron. One fox play and I'll irrigate your guts."

That old dragoon pistol, Fargo could see at a glance, had such a huge bore that even a hit to the limbs would prove fatal. They weren't called hand cannons for nothing. Cursing himself for a careless fool, he threw down his Henry and Colt.

"Now light down, Jayhawker, slow and easy. You spur that pinto, I'll kill it before you get ten feet."

"Oh, I b'lieve you'd kill anything on earth," Fargo replied as he dismounted, "if you'd kill Holly Nearhood."

Scooter smiled ear to ear, like a schoolboy being praised for good work. "Don't worry, she didn't go to waste. Don't ever believe, Fargo, that women don't fancy bein' raped at gunpoint. Holly, she begged old Scooter not to stop. Best poke she ever had, I'd wager."

Anger tightened Fargo's muscles, but he willed himself calm. He had promised to fix Scooter's flint for murdering Holly, but he needed proof—and now he had it.

"She looked so damned surprised, Fargo, when I sliced that soft white belly of hers open like a cheese," Scooter taunted, his huge form moving closer to his captive.

Fargo, his vision going red at the edges, said in a near whisper, "Thanks for the confession."

"Why, crusader, you a priest, too? Don't matter. Your ass is grass. You're gonna spend the rest of this night dyin' slow—ever had your hide peeled? Then comes the salt on all your exposed meat."

By now Scooter stood only a few feet away.

"My ass may be grass," Fargo replied, "but the blade you missed is steel, you woman-killing son of a bitch."

Fargo's long, strong legs had saved him before, and they did now. First his left leg sprang out hard, catching the hogleg and hurling it off into the darkness. An eyeblink later, in a well-practiced move, he lifted his right leg up and filled his hand with the Arkansas toothpick in his boot.

The muscles in his right shoulder corded like a bunched lariat as he made the killing thrust, adding the "Spanish twist" at the end. Fargo would far rather shoot a man than stab him, stabbing calling for a stronger stomach. But as he drove the long blade deep into Scooter's guts, he almost

112

enjoyed the release of body heat that washed over his hand. Scooter buckled to his knees, choking on his own blood, then flopped to the ground, twitching like a gut-hooked fish.

The last thing Scooter heard, before death claimed him, was Fargo's taunt close to his ear: "You're on your way to hell right now."

Fargo knelt to make sure the murderer and rapist had expired. He winced in disgust when he felt the neck for a pulse—Scooter's skin had the soft, pliant, greasy texture of uncooked bacon.

Cranky Man's sudden shout behind him made Fargo wince. "Fargo, where the hell are you? Dead? We're out of ammo and ready to—"

The Choctaw fell silent as he rode near enough to see a body on the ground. "Scooter Evans! Is he dead?"

Fargo stood back up. "Quiet as a fish on ice, if you take my drift."

"Do tell," Cranky Man replied scornfully. "And you giving all them pretty speeches how we ain't here to kill. Not that I give a shit, the skunk-bit coyote."

Fearing the occupants of the house would be emboldened by this hiatus in the attack, Fargo quickly dispersed the eight rounds in his Henry through several windows. By then the three Tutt men had joined them.

"Brother, what I'd give right now to be a frog in a pond of whiskey," Cranky Man complained as if nothing had happened. "Bourbon County, Kentucky, whis—"

"Stuff a sock in it, you fool," Fargo ordered, grabbing the Ovaro's reins and swinging up onto the hurricane deck. "We did good work, gents, but now we have to stick it out to the end. It's got to be done fast, in the next few days. We've still got Devil's Mouth to locate and the rest of the Evans clan to deal with."

He paused to give emphasis to his next words. "No laurels to be won. Just hard, bloody slogging. Right now let's raise dust. We could have Pukes down on us at any time."

As the men rode off in the pale moonlight, however, Fargo again heard a sound that stiffened the hairs on his arms: the savage snarling of wild dogs, seeming somehow meant for his ears.

13

The morning of Fargo's fourth day in northwest Arkansas found him waking up in Cranky Man's cave. "I don't like this," the Trailsman confessed over a cup of river-water coffee.

"Then don't drink it," Cranky Man bristled, living up to his name. "No skin off my ass."

"Not the coffee, you contrary fool. I mean leaving the Tutts alone."

Cranky Man dunked a wedge of ash pone into his coffee. "Sounds like you can't decide whether to go to church or stay home, white-eyes. Earlier, you said you had to avoid their place so the Pukes wouldn't attack."

Fargo nodded. "Your cave would be my first choice. But now that the Evans faction have broken the house truce, and the Tutts have responded, who knows?"

"Makes sense," Cranky Man agreed. "But don't forget, the Pukes are always night riders."

"Yeah, which should mean the Tutts'll be all right by day. But I'll be holing up in their barn nights."

"We," Cranky man corrected him.

"We?" Fargo repeated, surprised.

"Now, no need to mist up. *You* ain't worth a busted drum. But I like the Tutts, especially the old man."

Fargo grinned, but it quickly faded. "I was forced to kill Scooter last night, and we did fire and bullet damage to their house. It's going to be six sorts of hell around here. Especially when we go looking for that cave again."

"Do we have to find the damn thing? We know it's there. Can't we just tell the army?"

"Not yet," Fargo said. "State's rights keep them out of it until there's a federal angle, like with the bullion coach.

Besides, we need to know what's inside that cave. These Border Ruffians have been pillaging for years—hell, even your cave is filled with stolen property, and you're just one feebleminded half-breed. 'Magine what's inside Devil's Mouth."

"Feebleminded? Least I can top a squaw without having my horse stolen."

Fargo laughed. "You counted coup on me that time, red son. But we *are* riding back to that hill. No misdoubting that."

A few minutes later, as they rigged their mounts for the trail, Cranky Man said, "Things have changed since last night, Fargo. Sure, killers have been after you prac'ly since you rode into this area. But last night we didn't just stir up a hornet's nest—we *kicked* it."

"That was the point," Fargo said cheerfully.

"Sure. But what now? Every tree, every rock, every bend in the trail . . . that attack could come anytime."

Fargo, busy checking cinches and latigos, only smiled grimly. "So what? That's true every day of my life. Only way I'll ever die with my boots off is if I'm caught in bed with another stud's filly. Besides, out here there's no foolish 'duty to retreat' law like they got back east."

"The hell's that mean, duty to retreat?"

"British Common Law," Fargo replied as he started leading the Ovaro out of the cave into the rising sun. "I learned about it from a colonel at Fort Smith. Back in the land of steady habits, a man is supposed to run away when his life is threatened. Way I see it, that just leaves a killer alive to murder someone else."

Outside the cave entrance, Fargo shaded his eyes against the low sun. He had an excellent view of the hills, valleys, and Lead Hill.

"Just a few farmers stirring," he said after a careful study. "Let's dust our hocks."

The trail, at first, was wide and clear of screening timber. Fargo kicked the Ovaro up to a canter, a pace that made good time but spared the horse its wind and joints. Because of the drought, yellow plumes of trail dust rose behind them, bothering Fargo. It was damned hard to hide in water-starved country.

"Must be Sunday," Cranky Man remarked when they

saw a lone rider, dressed in clergy black, approaching on a long-eared mule. "That's a circuit preacher headed to Lead Hill."

"A Bible under his arm and no weapons," Fargo observed, not even bothering to knock the riding thong off the Colt's hammer.

As the slouch-hatted preacher rode closer, Fargo was even more reassured. Although fiery-eyed, he looked old enough to be straight out of Genesis. He had deep-sunk eyes almost hidden by wild eyebrows.

"Brothers!" the clergyman greeted them in a stern voice like the last trumpet, "don't you realize this is First Day morning?"

"First Day?" Fargo repeated.

"This is Sunday, sir, with the Lord's thumbprint still fresh on it. Don't you realize that Arkansas enforces breach of Sabbath laws?"

Fargo, like many frontiersmen who practiced no religion, strove to be polite to those who did.

"Well, Reverend, it's way too early for church," he objected. "So what's the breach?"

"My son, drinking, swearing, fornicating, even laughing are forbidden on Sunday. And I saw both of you laughing as I approached. I don't expect piety from a godless heathen"—his shrouded eyes cut to Cranky Man—"but you, Mr. Fargo, are in danger for your immortal soul."

A squiggle of warning moved up Fargo's spine. All of a sudden he whiffed the stench of brimstone, all right. Discreetly, he knocked the riding thong loose and palmed the butt of his Colt.

"Just curious . . . Reverend. How do you know my name? I've never met you."

Realizing his slip, the man's hand flew inside his frock coat and produced a Smith & Wesson from its canvas rig. Fargo's Colt was thumb-cocked before it cleared leather. Both weapons fired as one, but Fargo kept his wits and controlled his aim. His bullet punched into the would-be assassin's chest and wiped him out of the saddle. Fargo put a quick finishing shot in his head.

"Around here," he remarked as he leathered his shooter, "two's company and three's a riot."

"See?" Cranky Man demanded. "You can't even trust

preachers now, Fargo. You need to haul your freight back out to the western mountains. Arkansas will kill you."

"Why don't you put a tune to it?"

Fargo turned the mule loose and dragged the body off the trail. Not surprisingly, a quick search of his pockets turned up nothing informative.

"Preacher, my lily-white ass," he muttered. "Hired by the Evanses, the Pukes, or both. They sure set it up quick."

"Well, strike a light! He's finally figured out he's sledding on thin ice. You need to—"

"I ain't asking for advice," Fargo snapped. "I'm just thinking out loud."

"A neutered dog doesn't get it and neither do you. Right now you—*we*—are doing the hurt dance, Fargo. Death is here now, all around us."

"Nobody's stopping you from clearing out," Fargo reminded him as he stirruped. "Besides, my eyes sure won't miss you—a man could flip you into a pond and skim ugly for a month."

"In for a penny, in for a pound," Cranky Man said as he sighed in surrender and hauled up beside Fargo. "Let's go find Devil's Mouth."

"Right now," Fargo told him, "finding it can wait a bit. First we're going to take the temperature up on that hill and in the surrounding area. We're up against a criminal army, and we need to scout before we do anything else."

By midmorning sun broiled Fargo's neck and he turned up his collar. The wind, too, kicked up in gusts, blowing sand into his eyes like buckshot. He pulled down his hat against the swirling dust.

"Sheep clouds makin' up," Cranky Man observed. "Christ on his throne, Fargo, I think it might finally rain. Say! Why the hell do we keep circling that hill? The cave ain't down here."

"Why do you think?" Fargo riposted. "Have you forgotten that little reception committee yesterday? We need to know where every guard is before we head back up there. Besides, there's talk of an escape tunnel, and maybe it comes out down here."

"How many guards you spotted so far?"

"Just one, hiding behind a log. But I'd expect more. Anyway, we still need to take a squint at the surrounding country."

Fargo wasn't simply interested in Devil's Mouth. He intended to make a full, specific report to his friend Captain Dan Ridgeworth at Fort Smith on the state of lawless affairs around Lead Hill. As Hollis Maitland proved, the "constabulary" was unreliable. Some frontier peace officers were among the finest men Fargo had known; some others, however, would shame the devil in hell. The U.S. Army, while far from perfect, might be this region's best chance.

Thus, the Trailsman scouted in a wide loop, looking for sign. Just before the Missouri line Fargo reined in to study the ground under a group of spreading oaks.

"Lookit there where the grass was taken off by grazing horses," he pointed out to Cranky Man. "Right down to the roots. A good-sized group camped here at least a day or so. Prob'ly raided into Missouri."

Cranky Man, who had been watching for the ever-expected attack all morning since meeting the phony preacher, said, "Why hang around here with our thumbs up our sitters? They could ride back at any moment."

"I wouldn't put one red penny on it," Fargo said.

"Yeah? Well, I wouldn't put one *white* penny on your hunch. What makes you so sure they won't?"

Fargo led him to a nearby streambed where many riders had dug into the bed for seepage. "Not even a speck of mud—they turned up nothing. These bullyboy night riders can't afford to carry water for their horses—slows 'em down in a scrape. So they don't waste time at dry water holes."

Fargo, who had skipped breakfast, noticed how this little shadowed glade was literally hopping with rabbits. "Let's get outside of some grub," he suggested to Cranky Man, pulling a twig and some twine from a saddle pocket. "Best not to use a gun."

Fargo quickly rigged a snare, and in only minutes had caught a plump rabbit. He bled and rough-gutted it, then skinned it and spitted it on a sharpened stick.

"Not green wood, you ignorant savage," he roweled Cranky Man when the latter delivered some wood for the fire. "When you're hiding, always use deadwood—it doesn't smoke."

Fargo built a sparse Indian fire against a dirt bank, just a few sticks and handfuls of twisted grass, enough to singe the meat. The two men split the meal, washing it down with tepid canteen water. Thus fortified for the trail, Fargo led the way back toward the huge hill, on Evans land, where they suspected Devil's Mouth was located. This time, however, Fargo kept them off the trail, weaving through the pine, oak, and dogwood trees.

"Now *that's* new," Cranky Man remarked when the broad crown of the hill edged into view.

He meant the huge, seventeen-hand blood bay that stood among some saplings, its head down. The animal was not tacked.

"It's been cut," Cranky Man observed, meaning gelded. "And the tail and mane are trimmed, so it ain't wild. Maybe it's just a runaway."

Fargo, years of hard survival experience telling him to think otherwise, shook his head. "A horse is a naturally curious animal," he said. "It likes to look around. You see one that keeps its head down like that, he's either ailin' or somebody's tossed feed. I'd bet *my* horse there's at least one guard up there. Just hope it's the one we've already seen, and this is his horse."

"So what now?" Cranky Man groused. "We sit down here and watch your beard turn white?"

"No," Fargo said, "but we will watch things close before we head up."

More clouds piled up like boulders while they waited, hidden in the tall grass. Cranky Man flinched like a butt-shot dog when a loud whip-crack of thunder, so low and powerful it rocked the ground, startled both men.

"Nothing but heat lightning," Fargo said. "Won't rain much."

Fargo proved right. For perhaps two minutes rain came slapping down, barely enough to settle the dust much less ease the drought. Soon after the rain stopped it grew so quiet Fargo could hear the trees dripping.

"All right," he told Cranky Man, rising to his feet with his Henry to hand. "We waited because I had a hunch. Let's climb that hill and see if I'm right."

Fargo led them in a circuitous approach to the sentry post. By now he was sure there was only one guard up there—a curious fact in light of the importance of that cave. Unless Jimbo Powers and his Pukes were off raiding in force and planned to return soon—not too soon, Fargo hoped.

Even now he couldn't help noticing the peace and beauty of the hill. Twice Fargo stepped over quick-running streamlets, glimpsing the silvery flash and dart of minnows. He could hear big bass plopping in the deeper pools, reminding him of the fish line in his saddle pocket.

Years of survival discipline, however, kept his senses focused on that horse above. The guard wouldn't be too far away.

"There," he whispered to Cranky Man, pointing to a fallen log about fifty feet above them.

A Border Ruffian in a plumed hat rested with his back to the log, a big-bore Sharps propped up next to him. Fargo watched him crimp a paper, then shake some tobacco into it. He rolled the smoke and quirled both ends expertly.

More important, Fargo's hunch had been right. The Puke was imbibing from a bottle of potent mash and his head was starting to droop. His saddle sat before him in the grass and he ground his cigarette out on the saddle horn. A minute later he passed out in the grass, drunk.

"Hell, I can hear him snoring from here," Fargo said. "Let's go gag and tie him."

Neither man could have prepared for what happened next. The sleeping drunk's foot twitched, knocked over the Sharps Big Fifty, and the charged buffalo gun boomed like artillery when it struck the log. The fifty-caliber slug rocketed between Fargo and Cranky Man, tearing down saplings and peeling bark.

"Up and on the line!" the drunken Border Ruffian shouted as he came awake. "Jayhawkers!"

It all happened so fast that Fargo had no time to cover down. Drunk or not, the Puke got his Volcanic sidearm out in jig time and drew a bead on the intruders.

"Do it and you're dog meat!" Fargo warned. "We ain't here to kill you."

"Kiss my ass!"

Fargo swore at human stupidity as he shattered the man's breastbone with his first shot, tore open his heart with the second.

"His choice," Fargo muttered, nonetheless regretting that

he had been forced to kill. "And now there's been gunplay to alert the world. Let's take a quick squint up there, then hightail it."

Fargo knew, from his earlier visits, that it was the hilltop clearing, carved out by lightning, where the Pukes had concentrated before.

Suddenly the sound of a vicious snarl reached Fargo's ears on the wind.

"Wild dogs," Cranky Man said dismissively. "Sounds far off."

"No," Fargo corrected him, "not far off—muffled."

Fargo quickly realized why Devil's Mouth was so invaluable to criminals—he was so close to the entrance he could smell it, yet its location eluded him like a lost memory. It was Cranky Man, exploring behind some giant, mossy boulders, who finally raised a triumphant shout.

"Found it, Fargo!"

Fargo joined his companion and discovered why Devil's Mouth had eluded discovery for so long. The tumble of boulders appeared to lie flat against the hill. In fact, however, there was a generous gap between them and a cave entrance the size of a barn door.

"Darker than the inside of a boot," Fargo complained, stepping into the cool dampness.

He soon discovered that brass sconces had been drilled into the rock walls, each holding a fat piece of tallow candle. Soon dabbles of light were shimmering on the walls.

"Damn my eyes!" Fargo exclaimed. "The Pukes're running a hotel here. Not to mention a livery."

The cavern was the size of a very large house, one wall lined with bedrolls and heaps of personal gear. Piled-up rocks served as cooking stoves, and a beautiful, clear pool of water frothed up from one corner. What most caught Fargo's eye, however, were about twenty horses roped off in another corner. He also noticed a half-dozen or so mules with the U.S. brand on their hips.

"Say," Cranky Man fretted, glancing back toward the entrance. "Ain't we seen enough for now? All that shooting ruckus just now could have Pukes swarming down on this place."

"Just a minute," Fargo told him. "First, let's find this supposed escape tunnel."

"Let's not and brag we did. Them Border Ruffians would gut their own mothers for a chaw."

"To hear you take on about it." Fargo admonished, leading them toward the rear of the cave, "we came up here to do a nature study."

Both men clutching weapons, they began a systematic study of the smooth, striated rock. However, they discovered no opening for even a mouse, much less grown men and horses.

"Makes no sense," Fargo muttered. "Unless it's all hogwash about the tunnel."

"Let's clear out," Cranky Man urged, hopping up and down like he had to pee. "Ain't no damn tunnel."

"All right," Fargo agreed reluctantly, resolving to come back again. "At least we know where Devil's Mouth is. But first we got work to do."

Cranky Man complaining the whole time, both men quickly went through the stacks of personal gear, ruining every weapon they found by dashing them against rocks to destroy cylinders or barrels. Fargo collected up all the ammo and tossed it into the frothing pool.

"Now," he announced, untying the rope corral, "let's liberate this horseflesh."

Cranky Man threw down his greasy flap hat in frustration. "Fargo, what is wrong with you, and what doctor told you so? We were dead twenty minutes ago!"

"Then a few more minutes can't matter, you damned mission-school Indian. Haze 'em toward the entrance."

The horses, all tame but eager to be outside, hardly required any persuasion when Fargo, whistling and shouting, headed them toward the front entrance. As the first mount began fleeing down the hillside, however, shouts and gunshots opened up below. Bullets whanged off the boulders.

"Holy Christ!" Cranky Man panicked. "Fargo, you rabbit-brained idiot! The Pukes're back and here we are, stealing their horses. Are your *balls* made of brass or just your brain?"

"Shut up, you whiny old woman," Fargo snapped. "Bring that last bunch of horses up here."

"Christ, why bother? They've caught us—"

Fargo cursed as a ricocheting bullet threw rock dust in

his eyes. "The *horses*!" he repeated. "Ki-yi 'em on, damn it. With all the dust, that's our escape screen."

Catching on, Cranky Man reverted to his days as a wrangler and peeler, expertly funneling the last horses toward the hillside. Fargo, risking glimpses in the lead-buzzing air, saw the scene below was turmoil. As many as thirty mounted Pukes had been forced back by the headlong rush of escaping horses. Even better, the severe drought meant that a solid, yellow-brown wall of dust haze covered the hill.

"Now!" Fargo shouted. "You take the left flank, I'll take the right. Move fast while the dust is thick. We might get back to our horses without being spotted."

"What if they found our horses?"

Fargo's lips formed a grim, determined slit. "In that case, you can count on your magic pebbles—or save your last bullet for yourself."

Fargo's desperate plan worked. Both men made it to their horses unobserved in all the ruckus. The afternoon was still young, but Fargo figured it would be wise to hole up a few hours; so, staying off the main road, they headed across country toward the Tutt farm.

Up on the hill, Jimbo Powers and Clay Evans were fit to be tied. Powers had already lost a small fortune in gold when Fargo—he just *knew* it was that damned Fargo—notified Fort Smith about the bullion coach. Now some of Jimbo's best horseflesh was scattered across the Arkansas countryside, and his men would be days recovering them.

However, it was Clay who had a glint of murder in his dark eyes.

"That arrogant, meddling, do-gooder son of a bitch," he fumed, both hands caressing his Colt Navies. "First he cold-cocks me to impress that whore Mary Lou Tutt. Then he shoots up our house—*twice*, mind you—and murders my cousin Scooter. Now he's trespassin' on our land. This won't stand, Jimbo."

The leader of the local Border Ruffians nodded. His mouth quirked, not quite a grin. "It better not stand or we're sunk, all of us. But acknowledge the corn, Clay—he's a mighty potent force, right?"

"Horseshit! Not once has that lanky bastard offered to face me down in a draw-shoot. He's the type prefers to fight like an Indian, not a white man. Skulks around avoiding his enemy."

Powers, who had known of the Trailsman's reputation for years, silently disagreed with Clay. Evans was right on one score, at least: Fargo had to be stopped, and fast, or the game was over.

"I'll dance over his goddamn bones," Clay muttered, still watching the confusion on the hill. "At least the son of a bitch didn't find the escape tunnel—did he?"

Jimbo shook his head. "I spotted buckskins in all the dust. He wouldn't a run down the front if he knew about the tunnel."

Hatred twisted Clay's face. "It's time to call in the cards. C'mon, catch up your horse. We're takin' a little ride to the Tutt place. Just me 'n' you—leave your men here."

14

About a mile north of the Tutt farm, still avoiding the trail, Fargo raised his right hand to halt Cranky Man. He pointed to a tangled thicket on their left. The gray rump of a horse was visible through all the dead growth.

Fargo touched his lips to signal silence, then swung down and tossed the reins forward to hold the Ovaro in place. Cranky Man followed suit, both men sliding their rifles from their saddle scabbards.

The horse, Fargo was sure, belonged to Sheriff Hollis Maitland. But what was Maitland up to, this close to the Tutt property?

The two men crept around one end of the deadfall and found a surprising sight. Maitland, evidently drunk and a long way from his last shave, was sprawled on the ground with his head resting on a rock. A half-empty bottle of whiskey filled his left hand, and his right clutched his cocked six-shooter—which he was slowly turning toward his own right temple.

"Now, you just hold it right there, Hollis," Fargo admonished, stepping into view. "Having a high old time here, are you?"

"Huh. I'd have more fun watching paint dry."

"Well, life is short enough, you don't need to hurry it along. Lower your hammer."

"What will you do to me if I don't?" the star man demanded, his words slurred. "Shoot me? Hell, you'll be doing me a favor."

Fargo levered a round into the Henry's chamber. "Damn straight I'll shoot you—in the foot. You know what that feels like? Now toss that barking iron aside."

Cursing, Maitland did as told.

"The hell's this all about?" Fargo demanded.

"You really need to ask? It's about the fact that I've washed my hands of that goddamn, hell-spawned Evans bunch. I swear I never took part in their crimes—neither the murder of Holly Nearhood nor that raid on the Tutt's house."

"I believe you and so will others. Pull foot now, which you have, and you'll avoid prosecution. You're an elected local sheriff, not a federal marshal, and your power is limited. Nobody blames you, hell, the entire state is violent and crooked."

"Prosecution ain't the problem," Maitland lamented. "It's *execution*. By Scooter Evans, that sick son of a bitch. What he done to Holly was a bouquet of flowers compared to what he'll do to me once his uncle Langston turns him loose. The moment they snap to the fact I'm no longer helping them, Scooter is off his leash."

Fargo and Cranky Man exchanged a long look.

"Hollis," Fargo said, "Scooter Evans is feeding worms. I killed him last night after you left the meeting at the Evans place."

The sheriff looked skeptical. "Dead? Scooter?"

Cranky Man laughed. "Right now he's shoveling coal in hell. When Fargo kills 'em, they *stay* killed."

"That's mighty good news," Hollis agreed. "But it won't pull my bacon outta the fire. Clay and Dobie are reg'lar hellions, and Jimbo Powers and his Pukes are lickspittles for Langston Evans. Bad money drives out good, and the honest people with it. The thing is, I know too much, they can't let me live."

Fargo agreed the somewhat timid sheriff was in some deep sheep-dip. However, he was damned if he was going to let a basically decent man take his own life because of worthless human offal like the Evanses.

"You'll live," Fargo assured him. "Won't be long before the army will be coming into this, I'll see to that. Speaking on that: there's an officer at Fort Smith, Captain Dan Ridgeworth, same fella I telegraphed about the bullion coach. I've scouted for him on several expeditions into the Platte Valley, and we're good friends. One request from me, and he'll take you into protective custody until this shitstorm around here passes."

For a moment hope glinted in Maitland's bloodshot eyes. Then, shaking his head no, he struggled to his feet.

"Hell of a thing," he muttered gruffly. "A perfect stranger rides into Lead Hill, sees bad trouble, and puts his ass on the line to stop it. Meantime, the supposed sheriff hides behind the skirts of the U.S. Army. No, sir, this time I stand and fight. Just like Skye Fargo has been doing all his life—and always for the right side, I'd wager."

"Jesus," muttered Cranky Man, "Saint Fargo. He might save your hide, Sheriff, but he's doin' his damndest to get me killed."

Fargo had always admired brave men, but it was especially gratifying when a not-so-brave man found his hidden mettle. However, before anyone could say another word, a spate of gunshots rang out.

"Tutt place," Fargo said tersely, hitting a stirrup and swinging onto the hurricane deck. More shots rang out as he and Cranky Man heeled their mounts forward—followed by a woman's piercing scream that raised the fine hairs on Fargo's arms.

Fargo kicked the Ovaro to a gallop and speared the Henry from its boot, sticking the reins in his teeth while he jacked a round into the chamber. The Tutt place was only about a quarter of a mile ahead, but from the ominous silence he feared the damage was done.

"Shit!" Cranky Man cursed from behind him. When

Fargo glanced back, the Choctaw explained, "You ever try to gallop without a saddle horn? I need something between my legs!"

"Don't we all," Fargo muttered.

The moment he stopped speaking, Fargo saw a rider in a plumed hat racing toward them. He was so intent on watching his backtrail that he didn't spot Fargo until the Henry was trained on his lights. Fargo sent the man's hat flying, a warning to stop. Wisely, he did.

"Jimbo Powers," said Sheriff Maitland as he caught up, instantly recognizing the Border Ruffian from his bald head and sorrel horse. "Watch him, Fargo. He can be trickier 'n a redheaded woman."

"Strip his weapons," Fargo told Cranky Man. "Watch for a hideout gun. Then bring him back to the Tutt place."

The situation was pandemonium when Fargo reached the house. The commotion was out back, so he swung around the house and into the backyard. A grim-faced Jesse was cussing a blue streak while he saddled his horse. Joshua Tutt, his long Jennings rifle to hand, was staring into the surrounding woods, his face fierce as a Viking's.

Baylor lay writhing in the grass, blood oozing from a wound to his right thigh. A wooden water bucket lay in the grass beside him. Ma Tutt was snipping his pants away from the wound to get a look at it.

"The hell happened?" Fargo demanded, swinging down.

"Baylor was on his way to the well," Ma Tutt explained, "when *that* cockroach"—she pointed at Powers, just now arriving at gunpoint—"shot him. He meant to finish Baylor off, too, 'cept Jesse drove him off."

"Skye," Baylor hissed between pain-gritted teeth, "this ain't the half of it. Clay Evans nabbed Mary Lou. She was just headin' out to pick berries when Powers and Evans swooped down on us—*anh*!" he added in a harsh grunt when his mother touched the wound.

"You sure it was Clay?" Fargo demanded.

"It was so quick, I never seen his face. But it was Clay's black stallion, all right. He went through the woods 'steada takin' the road."

Fargo cursed silently. It was easier to track an ant across granite than to read sign in a leaf-carpeted bottom woods where ambushers could lurk anywhere. Best to assume it was Clay who took her—and most likely, to one of two places.

Fargo knelt to look at Baylor's wound.

"Bullet went clean through," Ma Tutt reported, relief in her tone. "I'll wash it out good with Pa's sippin' whiskey, then put a poultice on it to fetch any poison."

"I see you've had experience treating gunshot wounds," Fargo said.

"Huh! In *this* family? By now I could set up as a surgeon."

"You want me to take Powers and lock him up?" Sheriff Maitland asked.

"Just leave him here," Jesse said in a low, ominous tone.

Maitland shook his silvered head. "Sorry, son, your way is too harsh for the crime."

Fargo mulled it a few seconds, realizing that jugging Powers would be pointless. The "jail" in Lead Hill was nothing but a storage shed where drunks slept it off. Powers would be sprung by his men, and Maitland would be killed trying to win a lost cause. There had to be real law, with real courts, before justice could prevail.

Fargo spun toward Powers, who was still sitting his horse under guard. "Do you deny shooting Baylor in the thigh?" he demanded.

"I ain't denyin' a goddamn thing, Fargo," Powers replied smugly—perhaps relying on the Trailsman's reputation as a reluctant killer who never murdered.

Fargo, however, did not have murder in mind, just some Old Testament justice. Without a word, he raised the Henry's muzzle and shot Powers in the right thigh—exactly the same spot where the Puke had shot Baylor.

Powers' scream of pain startled the birds into silence.

"How do you like it now?" Fargo demanded. "Take the word back to your fellow desperadoes: from now on, you hurt one of ours, we *kill* two of yours."

He slapped the sorrel hard on the rump and it bolted off, its groaning rider barely hanging on.

"Fargo," Cranky Man remarked through a grin, "you'd drive a saint to poteen."

"Jesse," Fargo called, "never mind tacking that horse."

"Like hell I will! That sick bastard Clay Evans has got Mary Lou."

"All right," Fargo replied. "You go ahead and tear off like a Texas cyclone. And if you survive, maybe you can bury your ma and pa when you get home."

They were harsh words, but Jesse got the point—with Baylor laid up, Jesse was needed at home.

"*Sheriff* Maitland," Fargo said, emphasizing the word, "along with Cranky Man and me will go after Mary Lou right now. We'll start first with the Evans house before they can fort up, and we'll search the place from garret to cellar."

Fargo's greatest fear, as the three men lathered their horses toward the Evans place, was not hidden marksmen even though he knew they were out there. Rather, a gut hunch told him Mary Lou was now a captive in Devil's Mouth. That served two purposes: Evans, and no doubt others, would have their own white slave to slake their lust. Also, Evans was counting on a reckless rescue mission so he could kill the famous Trailsman.

Cranky Man evidently shared Fargo's hunch. At one of several stretches where the trail widened into a road, he heeled his skewbald up beside the Ovaro. "Fargo!" he called above the three-beat rataplan of galloping hooves. "Clay is scum, but he wouldn't likely put his family in the sights. You know where he prob'ly took Mary Lou, hey?"

Fargo nodded. "Look at it this way, chief. If we're right, we'll have to harrow hell to get her back. So it's best to first make sure we need to."

"Makes sense," Cranky Man agreed. He opened his mouth to say something else, but just then the road took a sharp dip. Cranky Man, forgetting he had no saddle horn, suddenly pitched forward off his horse, tumbling and bouncing in the thick dust. Sheriff Maitland's gray barely avoided running over him.

Cranky Man's livid cursing, as Fargo reined in and wheeled the Ovaro to ride back, told him the Choctaw couldn't be too badly injured. He rose from the roadside brush, dust clinging to him like pollen.

Fargo and Maitland exchanged glances, and then burst out laughing.

"Go suck an egg, both of you," Cranky Man growled. "I told you I had a round ass in the saddle."

"We need to get you a good saddle," Fargo said. "For now, try to stay in the one you got."

Cranky Man trotted after his nearby horse while the other men waited. Below the trail Fargo could see a valley plowed for crops. But the dwellings there were mostly hovels: a few brush shanties or crude wooden hutches with wagon canvas and buffalo robes for roofs.

"Newcomers who meant to build houses with the profit from their first crop," Maitland said. "The drought ruined their plans. Even if they somehow hang on for a better season, bad money drives out good."

"You hit the nail square," Fargo said, taking his meaning. "These folks are just a bunch of left-footed farmers. They work hard and don't lack courage, but as kill fighters they don't know sic 'em. They don't stand a snowball's chance unless the criminal trash is driven out."

Cranky Man forked leather and joined his companions.

"Rough piece of work ahead, gents," he said. " 'Specially if we gotta get Mary Lou Tutt out of that damned cave."

Fargo couldn't deny it, and since time was of the essence, he couldn't afford a subtle, safe approach to the Evans house. So the three riders simply waited until the final approach, and then rode all holler. They made the last yards behind a wall of covering fire. Fargo was able to kick open the front door before the startled occupants could return fire. It took mere moments to get Langston Evans, his hatchet-faced wife, and youngest son Dobie on a sofa in the parlor.

"Where's Clay?" Fargo demanded. "And Mary Lou Tutt?"

No one answered him. Three hostile faces stared at Fargo with a go-to-hell look. Dobie, busy with a razor and a strop, looked especially belligerent. Like his brother he had licorice black hair with a part down it straight as a pike.

"You're the murdering bastard that done for Scooter," Dobie finally replied.

"That honor fell to me, yeah." Fargo's long, strong right leg shot out, kicking the razor and strop from Dobie's hands. "I asked you three land-grabbing buzzards a question, and I expect an answer right about now."

"What's a matter, hah?" Dobie goaded. "Lose your poon, Fargo? Gotta skin the cat by hand now?"

It wasn't the Trailsman's habit to let criminals' insults

rattle him. He calmly stared down all three, everything in his face smiling except his eyes. He tickled the Colt's trigger in warning. "Don't blow smoke up my ass. I'm still waitin' on that answer."

This was too much for Langston Evans, who emitted a growl and heaved himself off the sofa to attack Fargo. Cranky Man stopped him cold with a short, straight-arm punch that split the patriarch's lips open and sent his meerschaum pipe sailing. Evans dropped back onto the sofa, so angry his face twitched.

"By eternal thunder, I *will* cook your hash, Fargo!" he bellowed through bloody lips. "You too, Cranky Man."

"Search the place top to bottom," Fargo told Maitland. "But watch yourself. I don't think Clay is here, but this place is a hive for criminal trash."

"Mister, you got it hindside foremost," Langston fumed. He pointed to the still-shattered windows and bullet-pocked walls. "*You're* the criminal, and if this tinhorn sheriff was any kind of man, you'd've stretched hemp by now."

Fargo hadn't expected any cooperation from the Evans clan, nor was he willing to force answers out of them—it would require torture. Besides, there was only one other likely place Mary Lou could be if she wasn't here.

"Evans," Fargo addressed the old man, "you can beat your gums till doomsday, it won't change the fact that you've fouled your nest. You've all got serious charges to answer for, including the murder of Holly Nearhood. My advice is to ease off instead of digging your hole deeper. Setting Mary Lou free would be a wise first move."

Maw-maw was chewing tobacco and spat with contempt, barely missing Fargo's boot. "You needle-dick bug-humpers don't scare us. Fargo, you *are* a fool. Struttin' around like a banty rooster, giving *us* advice! You're now taking some of your last breaths, frontier man. Nobody shoots his way into our home and lives to brag on it."

Maw-maw's reptilian eyes cut to Cranky Man. "Especially no flea-bit, gut-eating, turncoat savage. Cranky Man, you son of a bitch, we paid you good wages when you worked for us."

"Didn't know you were killers then. Money buys my labor, not my loyalty."

"Let it go," Langston told his wife. "The worm will turn.

131

These three will beg for death before Jimbo's boys are done with the slow knife work."

Maitland returned to the parlor. "Nothing," he assured Fargo. "I looked everywhere."

"You too, Hollis," Maw-maw said. "You turncoat son of a bitch. I personally will open you up from neck to nuts."

"On that gracious note," Fargo said, waving his friends outside ahead of him, "we'll take our leave."

"It's coming, Fargo!" Langston Evans roared behind them as they slipped outside. "A world of hurt, boy, that's all you got coming, hear?"

15

"So . . . what's tickin', chicken?"

These were the first words Clay Evans had spoken to Mary Lou since abducting her earlier. Now the two of them were alone in Devil's Mouth, and Clay was leading his stallion to the rope corral. Mary Lou trembled in every limb.

"Clay Evans," she fumed in a show of bravado, "it ain't too late to stop this foolishness right now. Just take me home and you won't be in no trouble, I'll see to that."

His sarcastic laughter echoed in the rock cavern, startling his stallion. Evans turned around and stood before her, solid as a meetinghouse. He was hatless, as usual.

"The cow don't bellow to the bull, sweet britches," he assured her. "Thanks to your sneaky stud, we got the whole cave to ourself while Jimbo's boys chase down the horses Fargo set free. And I aim to make good use of the time."

Mary Lou, in a desperate bid for time, said, "Skye Fargo found this place?"

Clay nodded, moving slowly closer to her as he shifted his shell belt. "Proud of him? Besides springing our remounts he ruint weapons and ammo. But it don't matter a jackstraw, see, on account I *know* your hero's gonna come here to rescue you. And before he does, I aim to get me a piece of tail. Drop your linen, girl."

Fear gripped Mary Lou so strongly that her mouth felt stuffed with cotton. Clay's eyes raked over her, taking in the blue broadcloth skirt, white cotton blouse, russet curls, and berry-juice eyes. Her hair in back hung in two thick plaits.

Mary Lou tried to defuse his sick lust. "Clay Evans, I *do* believe you're way too handsome to have to force a gal," she said in a playful, bantering tone.

Clay grinned, but without humor. "Takin' it is more fun. Strip buck before I *rip* them clothes off you."

Mary Lou was a master flirt and had perfected the art of blushing at will. She did so now.

"All right," she said coyly, loosing a button on her blouse. "You ain't a bad-lookin' fella. But don't get mad at me—I'm out with the flowers."

"Huh?" At first Clay looked confused. Then a look of suspicion settled into his features. "Oh, yeah, I take your drift. How do I know you ain't lying?"

Mary Lou knew she was on safe ground now. Most men of her day were squeamish about menstrual blood.

"Here," she invited him, starting to hike up her skirt. "I'll show—"

"Never mind that! How long I gotta wait?"

"I expect it'll be over directly—next couple days."

Clay resented this intrusion by Mother Nature. Except for a couple of sentries outside, he and Mary Lou had the entire cave. Jimbo Powers was getting medical help for his gunshot thigh in nearby Bull Shoals. His men who were not on horse-catching duty were hitting a federal freight caravan down south near Petersburg, Arkansas.

"So where's your new sweetheart?" Clay demanded.

"I might better go ask him," Mary Lou volunteered, starting toward the cave entrance.

A grip so strong it bruised her arm pulled her up short. "Just hold your taters, missy. Likely, he'll come to us eventually."

"After you've had your pleasure, you mean to kill me, don't you?" Mary Lou asked point-blank.

"Hell, that killin' talk was just anger speakin'," he said,

though his eyes fled from her probing stare. "You're here to draw out Fargo. Once he's gut-hooked, you can leave."

A skeptical dimple wrinkled her fair cheek. "A body might believe you 'cept you're such a bad liar."

"Go find a place to sit down," he snapped. "You're gettin' on my nerves."

You're here to draw out Fargo. As she selected a good place to sit along the back wall, she desperately hoped that would happen. Only a man of Fargo's mettle *might* be able to get her out of here. If he couldn't, Mary Lou knew she would die miserably—and more men than just Clay would enjoy her favors before he killed her.

She leaned one side of her head against the cool rock wall. Within minutes a muffled sound reached her ear, puzzling Mary Lou. Eventually she realized: it sounded like the vicious snarling of dogs.

Night was just starting to drag its indigo burial shroud across the sky by the time Fargo, Cranky Man, and Sheriff Maitland returned to the Tutt place. Since Maitland had refused Fargo's earlier offer of protective custody at Fort Smith, Fargo strongly advised the sheriff not to return to Lead Hill and almost certain death. Not just yet.

"Any news of Mary Lou?" Ma Tutt asked anxiously as she and her husband hurried out of the house to meet them.

" 'Fraid not," Fargo replied, and their hopeful faces fell.

"Get the dog far hence that's foe to man!" Joshua thundered like a fire-and-brimstone preacher. "Corinna's gone a-Maying!"

The three men on horseback exchanged quick glances.

"Anyhow," Fargo resumed awkwardly, "I'm almost certain she's a prisoner in the cave. And I got no plans to leave her there."

After inquiring about Baylor's wound, Fargo reluctantly turned down Ma Tutt's supper invitation—too much remained to be done and time was pressing. He, Cranky Man, and Maitland turned their horses out to graze, then climbed up into the hayloft to discuss the volatile situation. Fargo straddled a bale of hay.

"No way in hell we're going to storm that cave," he told his companions while he broke down the Henry to clean and oil it. "Even if we get lucky again and the men are gone, Clay could still kill her."

"How then?" Cranky Man demanded. "I'm just an ignorant savage, so spell this miracle out."

"We need one man who can get inside by invitation," Fargo replied calmly. "And since we ain't likely to find Pinkerton men growing in trees, I guess it'll hafta be me."

Cranky Man, who was keeping one eye on the road through the open loft doors, loosed a derisive hoot. "Fargo, does your mother know you're out? *By invitation?* Hell, you even *try* to make medicine with that bunch, they'll shoot you to mattress stuffing. Ain't many men look like you, they'll recognize you right off."

"If horseshit was brains, you'd have a clean corral," Fargo said. "Of course they'd recognize me unless I try a fox play. Baylor's my size—I'll shave, get rid of my buckskins, get a different hat. It's risky, but there's no way around it."

"What about the soldiers at Fort Smith?" Hollis asked. He kept his nervous hands busy softening his saddle with leather soap. "All it took was your name on a telegraph, and they got to that bullion coach in the nick of time."

"Sure, because there was a strong federal interest there. So far, all we know about inside the cave is a handful of government mules. Hundreds are stolen from the army every year, and it's hardly worth putting patrols in the field to track them down. No, we need more than mules before we can bugle the soldiers."

"Not to sound harsh," Hollis replied, "but it might already be too late for Mary Lou. Hell, you saw what Clay's cousin done to Holly Nearhood. First the rape, then the savage killing."

"No gainsaying that," Fargo had to concur. "But I don't think Clay's main reason for grabbing Mary Lou was to kill her. It was to lure me up there so he can kill Skye Fargo, the arrogant son of a bitch who thumped his ass in front of spectators. She may have been raped by now, but she might also still be alive."

"Makes sense," Cranky Man cut in. "But time is nipping at our heels. After you get your disguise all set, how you plan on crossing paths with the Pukes?"

"Yeah, I been giving that some thought." Fargo looked

at the sheriff. "Hollis, we spotted plenty of dust puffs earlier, rising from south of here. You got any idea where there's a good water hole around here—one the Border Ruffians like to use when they're returning from crime sprees in the south?"

Maitland pulled at the end of his beard-stubbled chin. "Well, with the drought and all, ain't too many. The best would be the one at Iron Springs—the water's hard from minerals, but it don't dry up even in droughts."

"Boys!" Ma Tutt's voice called from below in the barn.

Apprehensive, Fargo skinned his Colt and flew down the ladder. However, she only wanted to give him some sandwiches wrapped in cheesecloth.

"A body's got to eat," she scolded. "And if that don't stay your bellies, there's dewberry pies and cobblers cooling on the windowsill."

Fargo thanked her sincerely, for his stomach was rumbling like a thermal spring.

"Mrs. Tutt," he said, "any chance Baylor could lend me some of his duds? Preferably, stuff he hasn't worn in public lately. Shirt, trousers, and a hat would do. I also need some shaving gear."

Ma Tutt asked no questions. "I'll bring the things right out to you, Mr. Fargo. You know where the outside pump is—I'll bring you a looking glass, too."

"One problem, Fargo," Maitland said when the Trailsman had climbed into the loft again. "Your horse. The Pukes and Clay Evans will recognize it on sight. And any horse I or the Tutts might loan you would likely be recognized."

"Including mine," Cranky Man said.

"I been puzzling that out, too," Fargo said, handing sandwiches around. "I won't *have* a horse. I'll bring my Ovaro into the barn and leave him under your watchful eyes. One of you two will give me a ride to Iron Springs and leave me there. We just have to hope the Pukes follow their usual pattern of returning well after dark—and hope they let their horses tank up at Iron Springs."

"No horse?" Maitland repeated. "But then how—"

Fargo, busy chewing, waved him silent. When he'd swallowed he said, "Look, both of you, this rescue operation is dicey enough, I don't need reminders how many ways I might die before midnight. And I need to shave, change clothes, and get to Iron Springs before it's too late. It's close to dark now, so let's stow the chin-wag."

"All right," Cranky Man said, "but where will me and the sheriff be?"

"I hope you'll both be right here with Joshua and Jesse, protecting their family. Another strike on the house could come at any time and Baylor's laid up."

"So you'll just be on your own?"

Fargo chuckled. "I usually am."

Cranky Man and Maitland exchanged dubious glances, clearly worried that Skye Fargo would soon be hurled into eternity.

"All right, white-eyes," Cranky Man finally said. "Just one favor?"

He held up a clay calumet, used for ceremonial smoking by scores of tribes. It was already stuffed with kinnikinnick. "I know you ain't big on Indian magic, but I am. Will you have a quick medicine smoke with me to protect you and Mary Lou?"

Time was pressing, all right, but Fargo nodded—at the moment he needed any help he could get, supernatural or not. Both men smoked six times, one puff for each of the four directions of the wind plus the zenith and the nadir. The ritual, done solemnly, might please the cloud rulers of the cardinal points, for it emphasized the straight road to the center of the earth, symbolic of the straight path in life.

"All right, Fargo," Cranky Man said when they'd finished. "Roll the bones."

The sun didn't set—it just suddenly seemed to collapse, and all at once it was dark.

Fargo, dropped off at the water hole by Maitland, quickly checked for recent sign in the dirt at water's edge. A full moon, and a sky bursting with brilliant stars, lent plenty of light. Fargo gave a sigh of relief when he realized no riders had stopped there recently. They might not come, but at least he hadn't missed them.

He felt naked without his beard, and Baylor's homespun clothing felt alien against his skin. A floppy-brimmed hat served the valuable purpose of casting shadow over his distinctive blue eyes.

Fargo also felt naked without his Henry, but its brass frame had surely caught the eye of some of his enemies, so he'd left it behind. His single-action Colt, however, was a common model. Since this state was the home of the widely popular Arkansas toothpick, Fargo still carried his in its boot sheath.

Fargo had been taking his sleep in broken doses lately, and he was overdue for another dose. He was a light sleeper, so he decided to use this wait time wisely and catch a nap. After all, the Border Ruffians might not even pass this way tonight. If they did, he'd surely hear them in time.

Fargo found a sassafras thicket beside the moon-gleaming water and crawled inside. Despite his stretched nerves, sleep claimed him almost immediately. He had no idea how long he'd slept before the hollow drumbeat of many hooves woke him up.

Fargo sprang to his feet and glanced at the sky. He knew the moon generally looked white early in the night, golden when the night was well advanced. This moon was closer to golden than white.

The riders were in no apparent hurry, holding a trot and still about a quarter of a mile away. Fargo took his place beside the water hole and pretended to be drinking from his hands as the Pukes rode up in a clatter of bit rings.

No one assailed him, but they deliberately ruined the water hole for him by crowding their horses all around him—horses tended to urinate into the same water they drank, the main reason why men always drank first.

Fargo backed slowly away from the water, grim-faced men studying him closely. At least ten packhorses were connected to a lead line, no doubt hauling that day's booty. He knew that Jimbo Powers, whom he'd wounded earlier that day, wouldn't be up to leading a raid. However, Powers surely had several lieutenants, and one rode toward him.

"Mister, this is a mite queer," he said to Fargo, holding a shotgun on him. "Even hoors are gen'rally asleep by this hour. The hell you doin' out here with no horse?"

"Ask the half-breed Choctaw that stole mine," Fargo replied. "I mean to carve that fat bastard into jerky if I ever see him again."

"Half-breed Choctaw, huh?" The Puke's voice grew a bit less hostile. "I know the jasper you mean. If we get to him before you do, won't be much left to carve."

"Fine by me, just so he dies hard."

"How's come I never seen you around here before?" the Puke asked. "This area don't pull in many settlers nowadays."

Fargo deliberately paused, like a man hesitant to confess his deeds among strangers. "Well . . . you might say I had me a habit of lynching abolitionists in Kansas Territory. The law dogs up there are nigger lovers and don't favor such things. I skipped out just before they fit me with a rope collar."

Laughter from the ranks greeted Fargo's explanation.

"Lynching, eh?" the leader said, his voice friendly now. "Hell, that's right up our road."

A burly, full-bearded rider crowded up next to his boss. "Just hold your water, Butch," he told him, fierce dark eyes measuring Fargo. "This son of a bitch could be a Pinkerton man. He's got that fresh-scrubbed city-boy look to him."

The man swung down and belligerently shoved his massive chest into Fargo. He was taller than Fargo by several inches. "You don't look too tough to me, baby face. How'm I gunna know you ain't on Allan Pinkerton's payroll?"

"A real bullyboy, huh?" Fargo said. "How tough you want it, son?"

Fargo sent a looping blow toward the blowhard's jaw, connecting with a solid crunch. The Puke's eyes lost their focus and his knees came unhinged. He crumpled to the ground like an empty sack.

"*Hoo*-boy!" Butch exclaimed. "*That* was a sockdolager, stranger! Ain't nobody ever dropped Jack the Giant in one blow. Mister, what's your name?"

"Walt Mackenzie."

"Well, tell you what, Walt. We could use a jasper like you. Why'n't you come back with us and meet Jimbo Powers, our leader? I'd wager we can scare you up a good mount, too."

"Sounds jake to me," Fargo agreed, rubbing bruised knuckles against Baylor's trousers. " 'Preciate it, Butch."

Butch himself took Fargo up behind him. *Must have been*

that medicine pipe, Fargo told himself, for he could easily have died right there. Now, however, Fargo was going into the very belly of the beast—if and when it spit him back out, would he still be alive?

16

"Walt, your map sure looks familiar. Have our trails crossed before?"

"Might have, Mr. Powers," Fargo replied. "But if they did I don't recall it. I ain't one for remembering faces."

"Imagine Jimbo's face with hair over it," Butch suggested, and laughter rippled through the cavern.

"Pipe down!" Powers said, still watching Fargo thoughtfully—even a tad suspiciously, Fargo decided. That could turn ugly, especially since Fargo was the man who'd wounded him.

When the second half of the Border Ruffians arrived with their loot, Powers had been inside the cavern with the rest of his men. No doubt realizing they were all scavengers and looters, the wounded man came outside to supervise the arrival by dim moonlight. He used a billiard cue for a cane, wincing at each step.

At first the men slapped backs and bragged openly about their bloody deeds to the south, and Powers didn't notice Fargo.

"Had 'em a Cherokee wagon master," Butch told his boss, "so outta respect I waltzed it to'm with a tomahawk."

"A few a them barbers' clerks tried to fight, but we shot out their eyes, by God!" shouted another voice, followed by a cheer from his listeners.

Fargo generally riled cool. Even so, the bragging going on around him made him wish he had a handful of Cherokee Man-killers to help him settle accounts with these red-handed murderers. At least he now had solid grounds for contacting Captain Ridgeworth as soon as he could—those merchants attacked near Petersburg were under contract to supply goods to forts ringing the vast Indian Territory. That made the murders and the theft of goods serious federal crimes. Even better, the proof—rifles, sidearms, medicine, bacon, liquor—would be stacked in the cave.

However, the confusion of arrival was soon over, the goods stacked with the rest of their plunder. Now Powers was studying Fargo with the scrutiny of a physician. Fargo was grateful for the weak lighting, but suspected it wouldn't protect him very long. A man could quickly change his appearance, but not his voice, height, or build.

"Well, anyhow, glad to have you," Powers said. "Any man who can drop Jack the Giant with one punch and wants to keep the Africans in their place is more than welcome. You'll find blankets and such in the supplies. Get you some rations, too."

Powers was being civil enough now, but Fargo knew the mind worm of doubt would canker at him until he figured it out—at which point Fargo's life, and probably Mary Lou's, would be forfeit.

In fact, Fargo realized when he first glanced around the cavern, perhaps Mary Lou was already dead—or had not even been brought here, for he couldn't spot her or Clay Evans anywhere. Then he glimpsed a figure sitting in a dim recess in one of the walls. It had to be Mary Lou because Clay Evans sat guard nearby.

Butch caught Fargo watching her and grinned. "Looks like you got here just in time, Walt. Clay gets first whack at her soon's her monthlies have passed. Now me, I *like* the Red River Valley. But there'll be plenty to go around."

"Long as she's white," Fargo said, catering to the narrow views of his new "family."

"Lily white," Butch assured him. "C'mere. Every man needs to know about the escape tunnel."

Fargo's pulse quickened as he followed the Puke toward the back wall of the cavern.

"Clay!" Butch sang out. "Put the blinders on her!"

Evans covered Mary Lou's head with a blanket to protect their secret.

"This place used to be a robbers' roost back in the forties," Butch explained. "Back then, the tunnel was out in plain sight. One of the owlhoots who holed up here was a journeyman mechanic. Got him a stonemason to help him. Watch."

Butch handed Fargo the torch he was carrying and knelt down. "You'll find handholds carved out of the rock, just above the floor of the cave. Just put some muscle into it and lift."

Astonished, Fargo saw that an apparently solid slab of granite was actually a detached panel fitted with greased tracks. Butch slid it up about five feet.

Both men followed the tunnel for perhaps fifty feet. It was a crinkum-crankum, the winding and twisting reminding Fargo of the Snake River.

"This is far enough to show you what it's like," Butch said. He seemed uneasy about going farther, but Fargo didn't want to risk asking him why. "It comes out at the base of the hill, hidden real good by hawthorn bushes. Don't think we'll ever need it, but it's good to have an ace in the hole—get it?"

Both men laughed as they returned to the cavern to get some sleep.

"Wrap a lip around this, Walt," Butch said, pulling a flask from his hip pocket. "Moonshine made by old Langston Evans. Hoss, this liquor would make a rabbit attack a bulldog."

Fargo knocked back a slug and felt his eyes watering. "Christ, I'll be fartin' fire all night."

Butch laughed and thumped his back. "You're all right, Walt. Mind your pints and quarts around Jimbo, and you stand to get rich. We go equal shares on everything—and I do mean *every*thing. If Mary Lou Tutt's once-a-month time ain't over mighty damn quick, I'm takin' a gander under her petticoats to see if she's lying. Quiff is the one thing we ain't got plenty of."

Outlaws weren't usually big on discipline, but when Fargo rolled out of his blankets just past sunrise, many of the Pukes were already up and stirring. The massive cave entrance allowed plenty of light to stream in, and Fargo worried about Jimbo Powers' constant scrutiny of him. The man was edging closer to realizing that his worst enemy was now close enough to powder-burn him yet again.

Fargo helped himself to stolen army coffee and bacon, keeping his face slanted away from Powers. The Trailsman was grateful that two-gun thug Clay Evans was highly possessive—he rarely left Mary Lou's side, fearful some other hardcase would ravish his captive before Clay did.

"Walt!" Butch's voice sang out. "Got a little job for ya."

A lean, mean-eyed man with a typhoid tinge to his skin accompanied Butch. Fargo cast a glance at the pair of .44 army pistols, 1860 model, stuck into a bright red sash.

"Walt Mackenzie, this here is Travis Johnson, the best shooter Missouri ever sent a posse after. He can hit a dime at fifty yards."

Johnson's aggressive, stupid eyes took Fargo's measure. "Shootin' at dimes and bottles ain't quite the same as shooting at a man who fires back—am I right, Walt?"

"Right as rain," Fargo replied, acting deferential. The last thing he needed now was a clash of horns with another puffed up, two-gun bullyboy. Fargo had a mission, dangerous and near impossible, and every action he took should further that mission.

"Both you fellas are the new hands around here," Butch explained. "So that means you do some grubwork. The rest of us done it, too, in our day."

Fargo nodded; Johnson just sneered.

Butch went on, "There's a farmer on the Cross Timbers Road just north of Lead Hill. He raises chickens, too, got him three coops. Take some burlap bags, get us all the birds and eggs you can grab."

Jimbo Powers limped over, leaning on his billiard cue. His eyes bored into Fargo's. "That's *all* you do. No side trips to the saloon, no private heists for your own gain, just follow orders. We go equal shares, and that's a shooting point with me."

Both men nodded. Fargo was given a coyote dun gelding to ride, the famous lineback dun preferred by men who hazed cattle. He saddled it with a high-cantled cavalry saddle with wooden stirrups, also stolen.

"Pinchin' goddamn *chickens*," Johnson muttered when the two men were under way. "Why, Christ! Do you know that the famous Skye Fargo himself was hired to arrest me, for cuttin' timber on government land. Took him and five deputies to bring me in."

The absurd lie flattered Fargo, coming from an enemy. "On the square, Mr. Johnson? Then you'll soon be leading the Ruffians," Fargo assured him like a paid toady. "A man that goes heeled like you do, that's a man born to command, not obey."

Johnson couldn't help looking smug. "You said a mouthful there. Make yourself useful to me, and—*unh!*"

Fargo had waited until they were well out of sight of Devil's Mouth before sliding his Colt out and reining close enough to Johnson's horse to club the braggart with his revolver. The seven-and-a-half-inch barrel was not an ideal club, but Fargo laid it across the sweet spot on the side of the jaw and Johnson crumpled, then pitched sideways off his mount. Fargo heard a collarbone snap, but had no time to mollycoddle the criminal.

With no luxury for fancier plans, Fargo took both of Johnson's .44 pistols, along with a boot knife, and pitched them into the bushes. Then he tied him to his horse and raced to nearby Lead Hill. Luck was with him—Hollis Maitland's unimpressive jailhouse was unlocked and the key was hanging on the wall inside. Fargo tossed the prisoner, just now regaining awareness, onto the cot and trussed his hands and feet.

He locked the shed and pocketed the key, glancing around the sleepy hamlet. It was still early and he saw no one stirring. Fargo left Travis Johnson's horse tied off at the jail and made a beeline toward the Tutt Farm.

Hollis Maitland and Cranky Man recognized Fargo from the hayloft doors and pulled in their rifle muzzles.

"Fargo, you look like hell warmed over," Maitland greeted him out front of the barn.

"Funny, but somehow I can't relax when I'm trying to sleep in the bosom of bloody murderers," Fargo replied dryly while he hobbled the dun—it was a pretty good riding horse, but still skittish from abuse by outlaws, and Fargo was taking no chances with a runaway.

"So you bamboozled your way in?" Cranky Man said with admiration in his tone. "That explains the lineback."

"No time to rest on our laurels yet, gents. I'm in the gang now, yeah, but Jimbo Powers is on the verge of recognizing me. Mary Lou is all right, but those jackals will start raping her any time now. So we have to work out a break-out plan—for tonight. Hollis?"

"Yo!"

"I left a Puke named Travis Johnson in your jailhouse. I had to club him. Is the star man in Bull Shoals honest?"

"Not so's you'd notice. But we're pretty good friends. Why?"

"I recommend you hustle that prisoner over to Bull Shoals, and quick. His friends might track him down. Just trump up some charge. We need him out of the way before he can tell the rest of the Pukes I'm not on the level."

Maitland nodded. "I'll ride out as soon as we're finished here."

"That's not all we need at Bull Shoals," Fargo added. "I've got all the proof we need to bring in the army, but the telegraph lines around here aren't secure for this kind of damning information."

"What about that whatchamacallit, the pocket relay you used?" Cranky Man asked.

Fargo waved off the suggestion. "Takes too damn long to set it up, and I'm burning daylight as it is. Besides, even if I used the telegraph, soldiers can't get here in time to help me and Mary Lou. We'll have to get out on our own, tonight, and hope the soldiers toss a net around the Pukes. Skip the telegraph and use the messenger-express service I saw when I rode through Bull Shoals."

Fargo trusted the express riders. They were mostly just light, skinny kids, some only fourteen, but with an excellent record of delivery.

"Before you leave here," Fargo told Hollis, "I'll go up to the house and borrow paper and ink for the letter. That way it'll go directly to Captain Dan Ridgeworth instead of a telegrapher and a bunch of clerks."

"The yellowlegs." Cranky Man spat with contempt.

"They're all we got," Fargo reminded him. "The numbers are against us no matter if we fight like wildcats."

"What the hell is this?" Cranky Man carped. "Red man out? What about me?"

"Don't fret," Fargo told his Choctaw friend, "we all get a chance to die. At midnight tonight you and Hollis are going to the base of that hill. *Just* the base, hear? You're going to open fire toward the cave and keep firing as long as you can without getting nabbed. When they rush you, and they sure's hell will, I want you two to hit leather and get back here."

"What about you and Mary Lou?" Hollis demanded.

"No time to go into it, but we'll be on our own. With luck, you'll see us back here before sunrise."

The Trailsman hurried to the house, reported that Mary Lou was still unharmed, and wrote his note for Captain Ridgeworth. Fargo had an unpleasant task remaining when he returned to the barn, but it was the only way he might survive when he returned to Devil's Mouth without Johnson.

17

"I guess sunrise ain't the smartest time for stealing from a hoe-man. Dogs started howling to beat the devil, and the next minute Johnson caught a double load of buckshot, dead-on. Only reason I got away, the farmer had to break the gun open and reload."

Fargo finished his report and fell silent. A ring of unshaven, bloodthirsty cutthroats stared at him like an angry lynch mob. All looked suspicious of Fargo's tale, Jimbo Powers especially.

"But *you* miraculously escaped injury, hey?" Powers said. "Fess up, Walt: you're stretching the blanket a mite, ain't you?"

"I caught some whistlers, too," Fargo said, pulling up the left leg of his borrowed trousers. At Fargo's insistence, Cranky Man had used a hoof-pick to gouge a half-dozen bloody "buckshot wounds" in Fargo's calf. Several men whistled sympathetically.

"Damn!" Jimbo exclaimed. "Usually they just use rock salt on chicken thieves."

Fargo didn't have to worry about revenge against the farmer on Cross Timbers Road. There was no honor, or affection, among thieves. Rarely did they even bother to bury their dead.

Thus Fargo avoided a bullet and bought a few more hours of uneasy access to the cave. Now, however, Powers seemed more suspicious than ever, and Clay Evans had finally realized a new man was among them. Fortunately for Fargo, Clay rarely left his sentry spot near a despondent Mary Lou. Fargo was convinced she still didn't suspect the Trailsman was near, and he hoped to keep it that way.

Men left and returned throughout the day, but Fargo was the new man and assigned to laborious duty as hostler. The men left in the cave enjoyed a good hoisting session well into the night. Often the bottle was sent over to Fargo in the rope corral. He took gulps that were in fact sips, knowing he'd have to be clearheaded come midnight.

Fargo carried no watch, but the shifting color of the moon when he ambled outside the cave entrance, told him when midnight was fast approaching. He'd picked that time because he knew most of the men would either be drunk or asleep. Either way, they wouldn't likely make the best decisions when gunfire erupted—almost surely they would charge out front to defend their plunder.

Fargo had just started to turn around and go back into the cave, after his latest check of the moon, when cold steel kissed the back of his neck. A hammer clicked, and Fargo froze like a hound on point.

"Turn around *slow*, you sneaky bastard," Clay Evans' voice hissed in a low threat. "I suspicioned you the minute you got here. Let's have a look at your face."

Fargo knew he was trap bait once Clay raised the alarm—and before long, Mary Lou with him. So he didn't debate his actions, but struck immediately, spinning hard to the left. His left arm knocked the Colt Navy from Clay's hand before he could fire; Fargo continued spinning as he drove a powerful right cross to Evans' granite jaw.

That blow landed loud and rocked Evans back, but Fargo took no chances, delivering rapid, hard one-two punches even as the big man folded to the cave floor, unconscious.

It happened so quick that the few men still awake had no time to step in. Butch and Jack the Giant were playing cards. They hurried over, hands palming the butts of their belt guns.

"The hell was *that* all about?" Butch demanded. "Looked like he jumped you from behind."

"He did." Fargo spread his arms, the picture of innocence. "Damned if I know why. This jasper said I was eyeing his woman and he was gonna kill me."

Butch and Jack exchanged knowing glances.

"Clay's what they call a dog in the manger," Butch said. "You know, got him a juicy piece of meat that he won't eat and he won't share."

Jack the Giant grinned at Fargo—this now made two men Walt had beaten unconscious. "Well, Clay's out good now," Jack said. "I say let's check and *see* if that uppity bitch is on the rag. If she ain't, I say we got first dibs."

"Boys," said Butch, rubbing his hands together, "black your boots, we're goin' on a tear!"

Fargo saw his makeshift plan going to hell fast. Just then he was saved by the sharp crack of repeating rifles suddenly opening up below the hill, shattering the stillness of the night.

"Christ! Jayhawkers!" roared Jimbo Powers, torn out of sound sleep. "Up and on the line!"

All was pandemonium inside the cave. Men, half drunk and half asleep, grabbed their weapons and raced out front, a newly recovered Clay Evans among them. Cranky Man and Sheriff Hollis were doing a good job of sustaining fire, but Fargo knew the Pukes would quickly realize this was not a large force. He had to work fast.

Unnoticed in the confusion, he ran toward the niche where Mary Lou sat on a buffalo robe. Seeing him, she opened her mouth to scream.

"Shush it, girl!" Fargo warned. "It's Mr. Buckskins without his buckskins."

Out front, weapons fired so rapidly it was one continuous crackle. Fargo swiped an army carbine propped near a bedroll, then grabbed Mary Lou's hand and pulled her toward the rear wall. He slid the cleverly mounted granite slab up, revealing the dark maw of the tunnel.

"Skye! What—"

"Stow it, girl, every second counts. Here, take this."

He handed her a torch and tugged her into the tunnel,

sliding the panel shut behind them. He thumb-scratched a lucifer into flame and lit the torch.

"We got damn little time, hon," he explained, hurrying her along. "They won't miss me right away, maybe, but they will you. They'll come after us at both ends, so we *have* to get out of here and safely into cover before they trap us."

Left and right the narrow tunnel twisted, and Fargo knew trouble lay ahead when he felt his scalp stiffen in warning. For a moment he thought he heard low, menacing growls. However, he realized they had to charge ahead full-bore, dangers be damned—shouts, then shots, behind them in the cave meant they'd already been discovered.

All the twist and turns should have protected them from bullets. Instead, the hard granite walls made for a deadly ricochet chamber. Bullets whanged in all around them, whining past their ears. Fargo pushed Mary Lou out in front of him to shield her.

He hated to waste lead, but Fargo had to assume some Pukes were following them. He aimed the carbine and heard the hammer click on an empty chamber—like a greenhorn he'd failed to check the magazine.

Fargo skinned his Colt and sent six slugs skipping behind them. A scream from Mary Lou swiveled his head full-front, and Fargo felt his skin go clammy.

Vicious yellow eyes glowed in the torchlight, and wicked fangs dripping saliva. Perhaps a dozen wild dogs, a few clearly rabid, hunkered in the tunnel. Rancid meat had been tossed to them, and gnawed bones lay everywhere.

Now Fargo understood why Butch hadn't led him farther inside when showing him the tunnel—the dogs didn't come close to the tunnel entrance, but stayed halfway down. The Pukes must have fed the dogs just enough to keep them around, knowing they wouldn't attack large groups—but isolated intruders were fair game. It saved on sentries.

Mary Lou screamed again, and Fargo slapped her to quell the hysteria.

"Don't let them know you're scared," he snapped. "Let's get in the first blow."

Remembering Mary Lou was good at reloading weapons, Fargo stripped off his gun belt and gave it to her. "Load my six-shooter," he told her. "And stay behind me."

Even as Fargo finished speaking, a huge yellow cur leaped for his throat. Fargo used the short carbine as a club, cracking the dog solidly across its muzzle. Pieces of teeth flew everywhere and the dog howled piteously before racing into the darkness behind the pack.

But that didn't scare off the rest. Growling savagely himself, Fargo clubbed, kicked, even picked up rocks and hurled them. The dogs alternately cringed back, then lashed forward. Fargo was relentless in his attack, knowing that if one of those rabid curs managed to bite him or Mary Lou, they were gone-up cases. Turning back was no option either—ricocheting bullets still rang off the rock walls.

Mary Lou's trembling fingers finally got the Colt loaded and she thrust it at Fargo. By the time he'd shot four dogs, the few remaining tore out of the tunnel.

Fargo and Mary Lou rushed forward, feeling the first cool drafts that marked the lower opening.

"There's shooting down here, too," Mary Lou said. "Have they gone around to cut us off?"

"'Fraid so," Fargo told her as he thumbed four reloads into the Colt's cylinder. "I only told Cranky Man and Hollis to shoot from the front of the hill. I figured we'd get out in time, but I didn't count on those damn dogs slowing us up."

"So what will we do, Skye?"

"Face it, even though it's ugly: I'll be killed. Worse, you'll be raped repeatedly before you're killed. So there's only one thing we *can* do."

"You mean . . . ?"

"I mean we don't stop, no matter what. We can't. I aim to die fighting."

"Me too," she said resolutely. "I druther die with you than let Clay Evans touch me. That's worse'n a bullet."

"There!" Fargo said, spotting a patch of starry sky ahead. "We're almost outside."

"Laws," Mary Lou fretted, "listen to that gunfire."

Fargo was indeed listening, and something was odd about all that shooting. Why would Pukes be firing so madly before he and Mary Lou even emerged? Besides, no bullets were striking near the tunnel's exit; instead, the fire seemed directed toward their left.

They reached the hawthorn thicket at the tunnel's end and Fargo cautiously poked his head out.

"I'll be damned," he muttered. "Those two reckless fools didn't listen to me."

His tone was filled with admiration for Cranky Man and Sheriff Maitland. Instead of staying around front, as ordered, they had circled around the hill to cover Fargo and Mary Lou's escape. Perhaps a half-dozen Border Ruffians were crouched behind cover, returning fire.

"Their backs are to us," Fargo whispered to Mary Lou. "Let's get to safer cover."

Fargo took Mary Lou's hand and they headed off to the right of the big hill, where a huge wood offered cover. Just then, however, a Puke glanced back and saw them. He gave the hail to his comrades, and the running gun battle was on.

Fargo had reloaded but had only six shots. He was able to return only one bullet for every six tossed at them. Nor could Mary Lou run any faster—she'd been sitting, legs cramped up, since her capture. The Pukes were gaining and their slugs hissing in closer.

Abruptly, a deep, ferocious bellow was followed by the hollow drumbeat of galloping hooves. Fargo aimed a cross-shoulder glance to the rear and felt his heart swell: Sheriff Hollis Maitland, his face wild in the pale moonlight, bore down on the running Pukes on his big gray. Cranky Man followed in his wake, repeating rifle belching fire.

Several Pukes cried out, wounded, while the rest went to cover. *Go back now, Hollis,* Fargo urged silently, still watching over his shoulder as he and Mary Lou fled. *Now, you gutsy son of a bitch!*

The next second, however, Hollis threw both arms out toward heaven and rolled off his horse, shot fatally in the head. Cranky Man, lead thickening the air around him, reversed course and lit a shuck to the north. But both men had accomplished their heroic suicide mission: Fargo and Mary Lou had made the relative safety of thick woods where horses couldn't go.

Fargo, no man to mist up easily, felt a trembling heat behind his eyeballs. He recalled Sheriff Maitland's words when he had refused protective custody at Fort Smith: *Better to buck out in smoke than live your life running scared.*

It was one thing to make mistakes out of fear for his life; another altogether to redeem himself in blood as he had just now. Hollis Maitland's awesome bravery might have come late, but it was just in time to help save two lives.

"Guess I had the wrong idea about Hollis," Mary Lou said as they pressed deeper into the dark cover of the woods. "Laws! He had them Pukes scared spitless."

"He'll rate aces high with me until my dying day," Fargo vowed. "Whatever he did wrong, he squared accounts with the price of his own life. Right now, though, we've got to use the precious time he bought us and hole up somewhere safe. They'll beat the bushes on foot for a while, and then give up. We can't be moving right now in all this underbrush, they'll hear us."

"He ain't the only hero," Mary Lou insisted, squeezing Fargo's hand. "Clay kidnapping me was just like Pluto kidnapping Persephone. And you came right into hell to save me."

"That's a mite fanciful, lady. Besides, life ain't no Greek storybook—do you hear them shouts behind us? They're organizing a search line. Your 'happy ending' is still a ways off. Now shush up and keep your eyes and ears peeled."

18

For perhaps an hour Fargo led Mary Lou deeper into the tangled growth of the woods, using the polestar to keep him generally on track toward the Tutt House. Pursuit sounds were confusing—one moment behind them, the next moment on one of their flanks. Snarling noises bothered Fargo, too. The fleeing wild dogs must have headed this way.

"Lands, Skye," Mary Lou complained at one point, hanging back from sheer depletion. "I'm powerful sorry, but I'm most dead from exhaustion. I didn't sleep a wink in that dang cave, nor hardly eat. I'm plumb done in."

"Sure you are," Fargo agreed sympathetically. "Since they aren't using hounds, our best bet is to find a good hiding place and hole up until they give up the search. This is a big stretch of woods."

Fargo had never missed the Ovaro more than he did that night. The stallion could negotiate any terrain, including dense woods in the dark.

"Hold it," he told Mary Lou, spotting a big, hollow log in the scanty moonlight. "That just might do it. They've saved me before."

"That old dead *log*?" Mary Lou protested. "Skye, anything could be inside there. Snakes, black widows—"

One of the Pukes shouted to a comrade, only a hundred yards or so behind them.

"Never mind," Mary Lou amended herself quickly. "Let's crawl inside fast."

It was a tight fit for both of them, Mary Lou because of her voluminous clothing, Fargo because of his street-wide shoulders. He helped Mary Lou back herself into the log first, and then backed in himself.

Insects of all sorts did indeed crawl all over them and cover them with bites. However, Fargo was glad he'd decided to hide: shouts from ahead and behind proved the Pukes had formed two search lines and were closing the net.

"Will they look in here?" Mary Lou whispered from behind him.

"I doubt it," Fargo reassured her. "An Indian would, but white men search different. They'll ignore the ground and concentrate on thickets and beating the bushes."

"Hope you're right," she whispered. "They're thrashing closer."

Fargo's arms were pinned so tight that he couldn't draw, or even fire, his Colt. It didn't matter, given the numbers pitted against them. Moments later, however, a dog snarled nearby, and Fargo felt a cold hand squeeze his heart.

Those damn wild dogs! One must have caught their scent and was approaching the log even as the men did. Now it began barking and snapping ferociously at the opening only two feet from Fargo's face.

"Up here!" shouted a voice he recognized as Butch's. "One a them wild curs has caught a scent!"

Now they'll look inside, Fargo realized. Men thrashed closer and the dog ran off—but not before the damage was done.

"He was barkin' at that log," the voice of Clay Evans said, almost on them now.

"Aw, hell," Butch said. "Prob'ly just a coon or possum."

"Let's peek inside anyhow," Clay retorted. He raised his voice: "Fargo, the death hug's a comin', you hear me? It's *over*, boy! You got me savage mad now, crusader!"

Fargo heard a hammer click and deeply regretted that he could not at least take Clay out before his own wick was snuffed—with his arms trapped by the log he couldn't even draw his shooter. Fargo found one ray of hope: the Pukes had run out of the cave so quickly that they grabbed no torches. The moonlight, dim at best, barely penetrated the opening of the log.

Men stopped near the log even as Fargo forced himself and Mary Lou farther back from the opening. Knowing his smooth-shaven face would reflect light, Fargo kept it turned away.

"Hey, Fargo," a soft voice called into the log, "I see you, cock chafer. C'mon out, and bring my poon with you."

Fargo refused to rise to the bait. A moment later, however, a lucifer scratched to life, and Fargo felt his scalp tingle.

"Shit!" Clay swore when a sudden gust of wind blew out the match. "That's my last phosphor."

"I can't see a damn thing in there," Butch's impatient voice said, so close to Fargo's ear the Trailsman flinched. "We're wasting time."

"Yeah, but just in case . . ."

Fargo guessed what was coming, but had no way to warn Mary Lou. The best he could do was trap her head between his boots and press it flat. An eyeblink later Clay's Colt Navy belched fire and smoke, the bullet raking a line of fire across Fargo's back. The detonation, in that confined space, left his ears hurt and ringing.

"If he *is* inside there," Clay gloated, "he ain't goin' nowhere."

"C'mon!" Butch urged. "They're running, not hiding in logs."

Fargo's back burned, but experience told him the wound was just a crease—a lucky crease. An inch lower and he'd literally have a hole in his head. Acrid powder smoke filled the log, and he felt Mary Lou struggling not to cough.

He waited until the searchers had moved on, not uttering a sound. Finally, heart stomping with nervous fear for Mary Lou's safety, Fargo asked, "You all right?"

"I—I think so. And you?"

"Considering I'd *ought* to be dead," Fargo replied, as he wiggled out of the log, "I'm fit as a fiddle. They're all ahead of us now. Let's give them time to finish up here. We'll hole up in a new spot until they leave, then clear out of the woods and hightail it to your place."

He helped Mary Lou out, brushing insects and spiderwebs off her clothing.

"My house?" she asked. "You're thinkin' they'll attack there again?"

"Distinct possibility," Fargo assured her. "They favor sixshooter persuasion. But don't forget—it cost them dear last time they tried it, and they might not. If Cranky Man made it back in one piece, that's four guns, assuming Baylor is able to fight. They'll need all the help they can get."

Right now, though, Fargo still heard faint shouts out ahead of them. He and Mary Lou took shelter under a tangled deadfall. Fargo figured it should be safe to leave in about an hour.

"Clay nor none of the rest ever raped me," Mary Lou told Fargo proudly. "Told 'em I was out with the flowers."

"Are you?"

She smiled, well-formed teeth gleaming like pearls in the moonlight. "Why'n't you find out, Mr. Buckskins?" she invited, a teasing lilt in her voice.

"I thought you were so tired?"

"I am," she said, fumbling at the cowhide belt holding up his borrowed trousers. "But just think, if we get killed, we'll never do this again with anybody. Plus, I just found out that danger, once it's over, is mighty . . . exciting."

She freed his straining manhood and drove Fargo crazy with pleasure when she stroked it in her tight, squeezing fist. Her free hand slid her pantaloons down around one ankle.

"Put it inside me, Skye," she begged in a husky whisper. "I'm gonna milk you for every last drop."

Fargo, his Colt ready to hand, gave up his feeble resistance and rolled between her shapely legs.

Well before sunrise the search noises stopped.

"Strange," Fargo remarked as he stared at the low glow in the eastern sky, known as false dawn.

"What's strange?" Mary Lou's voice sounded sleepy—their only rest had been an uneasy nap after they made love.

"I didn't hear any riders leave the cave. Even if they decided against attacking your place, why not comb the roads and trails for us?"

"From what I heard them slaver criminals boastin' inside the cave," Mary Lou opined, pulling twigs out of her hair, "they ain't scairt of nothing. Government, law, ain't nothin' gonna stop 'em. Far as us gettin' away—Clay Evans knows he only has to wait till you ride on, and then he'll nab me again. Only, next time he'll make sure I don't get away."

"He might be thinking along those lines," Fargo agreed. "But all the cards ain't been dealt yet. C'mon, let's head for your farm."

It was about four miles to the Tutt farm, a difficult trek because they avoided roads. The new sun was a dull orange glow behind the hills when they finally reached the yard gate.

"A sight for sore eyes!" Cranky Man greeted them from the roof of the house, where he'd been standing guard. He climbed down while Joshua, Jesse, and Ma Tutt ran outside and practically mobbed Mary Lou. Baylor limped out behind them, all smiles. He pumped Fargo's arm.

"We're still a long ways from Fiddlers Green," Fargo cautioned amidst this happy reunion. "Jimbo Powers won't be afraid to strike this place again, not if his feathers are ruffled about last night."

Cranky Man's moon face was divided by a grin. "Jimbo Powers ain't worried about a damn thing, Skye, 'cept maybe the temperature in hell. I killed him last night when he led the charge down the front of the hill. Damn fool was limping and made an easy target."

"That explains the lack of action," Fargo said, nodding. "These militia bands don't have a clear line of authority and tend to elect their leaders. They'll take care of that before they launch any new crimes. Given that bunch of hotheads, they'll need time to settle on a name."

"But Clay's not one of 'em," Mary Lou interjected. "Him and his brother Dobie might round up some of their no-'count cousins from the outlying hills—includin' Scooter's brothers."

"Distinct possibility," Fargo agreed. "Far as that goes, the Pukes could already have a new leader and hit your house tonight. We have to be ready day and night. It's all coming to a head now."

However, for the rest of that long day and throughout the night, all was calm. The following sunrise brought a sudden commotion of distant noise: a bugle sounding the cavalry charge, followed by a ferocious gun battle.

"Hollis did it!" Fargo exclaimed, elated. "He took my note to the express riders in Bull Shoals. Now the army should find enough evidence to jug those Pukes for murder and theft of government property."

Less than an hour after the battle noises fell silent, a lone cavalry officer in a snap-brim hat trotted up to the Tutt house. Fargo, busy currying the Ovaro out in the barn, strolled out to meet him. So did the entire Tutt family.

"Captain Dan," Fargo greeted his old friend. "All secure?"

"Thanks to you, Skye," Captain Dan Ridgeworth replied. "I've always been able to count on your field reports, and this one was no exception. We covered both entrances to that cave. The ones who resisted were killed, the others arrested. More than half chose arrest, and I'll guarantee you they *will* rot in prison. They're going before a strict magistrate."

"I've heard of him," Fargo said. "Judge Winslowe Collins, a strong Union man. What about the Evans family I mentioned? They're pure poison."

Captain Ridgeworth shook his head sadly. "*That* bunch hasn't got the good sense God gave a turnip. I sent a squad there just to search the house since Clay was under arrest at the cave—that gave me jurisdiction. Those ornery idiots opened fire on my men. They found out in a hurry what ten sharpshooters fresh off a battle can do. The old man and Dobie were both killed, the mother seriously wounded."

At the memory of Maw-maw Evans, Ridgeworth visibly shuddered. "Actually, 'mother' is a stretch for that harpy. Jesus, is she a mean one. Tried to kick me in the nu—"

The officer glanced down at Ma Tutt and Mary Lou. "Ah, in the groin region, I mean."

Ridgeworth recalled something else and looked at Fargo again. "It was the darndest thing, Skye. At the cave, at least a dozen of those Border Ruffians tried to make a break for it as we approached, Clay Evans among them. Might've got away, too, but every one of them was bucked off his horse."

Fargo flashed a sly grin. "Proud to say I had a hand in that. I was the new man, and they put me in charge of the horses. You know how outlaws tend to leave their horses saddled for a quick getaway. And you, bein' a cavalryman, known damn well what happens when you girth a horse too tight."

Ridgeworth laughed. "Either he'll buck you or you'll gall it."

"Yeah, and these being mistreated horses, they chose to buck."

Mary Lou, abrupt tears of joy spurting down her cheeks, took Skye and Ridgeworth's hands at the same time. "God bless you both—and Cranky Man and Sheriff Hollis, too, may he rest in peace. The Pukes *and* the Evans bunch gone! As long as there's brave fellas like you around, decent folks got a chance."

Fargo refused to point his bridle west again until he saw that Sheriff Maitland had a Christian burial. The little cemetery atop Lead Hill was crowded, for news of the sheriff's gutsy charge against certain death had spread far and wide. Fargo stood among the solemn Tutts and damn near misted up all over again when the circuit preacher declared solemnly, "Hollis Maitland taught us a simple lesson: a man brave for even one second can change the course of history."

As Fargo, Cranky Man, and the Tutts turned to leave the cemetery, a gratifying sight met their eyes: a tumbleweed wagon, as prison vans were called, was creaking through Lead Hill with the last of the prisoners, hauling them to Fort Smith. The spectators broke into spontaneous cheers and applause.

"Mr. Fargo!"

The Trailsman glanced left. A newspaper photographer, in a derby hat and bright paper collar, squeezed the bulb in his hand and a flashpan filled with magnesium powder exploded in a puff of smoke. Fargo started to cuss, glanced around at the headstones and crosses, then checked himself.

"Looks like you're a hero again, Fargo," Cranky Man roweled him. "It'll get you more lead to pick outta your ass while you head west."

Fargo grinned good-naturedly. "What about you, old son? I tossed your bar-key. But that cave of yours is full of stolen goods. You got plans to walk the straight and narrow?"

Cranky Man shrugged. "The coals have turned to ashes for my people, but I'm returning to the Indian Territory. I see you white people have one hell of a war coming over this damned slavery mess. It's none of my picnic, and I better clear out before the cannons boom. Do you mind company on the first leg of your trip to Pikes Peak?"

"Not if you plan to stay stinking drunk the whole time," Fargo shot back.

"Drunk?" Cranky Man looked offended and switched to his high-hatting manner. "It's true that I take frequent potations from a bottle, but I'm certainly no drunk."

Fargo gave in, laughing. "Glad to have you along, friend. And you're dead right about that war coming soon. Americans'll be lucky to still have a country when it's over."

Fargo said his good-byes to the Tutts. Old Joshua gripped his hand an extra few seconds. "Good-bye and God bless . . . Mr. *Fargo*," he said, getting the Trailsman's name right for the first time.

As Fargo and Cranky Man crested Lead Hill, beginning their journey to the buffalo plains, Fargo reined in and slued around in the saddle for one last look.

This pretty country of hills and valleys, of steep razorbacks and lush bottom woods, was deceptive. Someday it would be a hoe-man's paradise. Right now, though, all the violence of any wild frontier, as well as the simmering tensions of slavery and impending civil war, made for a volatile mix.

"If I owned hell and Arkansas," he told Cranky Man, "I'd rent out Arkansas and live in hell."

Fargo thumped the Ovaro with his heels, trailing the westering sun.

LOOKING FORWARD!

**The following is the opening
section of the next novel in the exciting
Trailsman series from Signet:**

THE TRAILSMAN #297
SOUTH TEXAS SLAUGHTER

*South Texas, 1860—where danger and death lurk
in the thorny thickets of the brush country.*

Leaning forward in the saddle as bullets whistled around
his head, the big man in buckskins urged his stallion forward. The magnificent black-and-white Ovaro responded
gallantly, as he always did, stretching his legs as he galloped
along the winding trail through the chaparral.

Skye Fargo cast a glance over his shoulder, his lake blue
eyes narrowing as he saw his pursuers race around a bend
in the trail and thunder after him. The guns in their hands
spouted flame. Lucky for Fargo, it was difficult to aim very
accurately from the saddle of a galloping horse.

Running away stuck in his craw. It was his way to stand
up to trouble whenever, wherever, and however it con-
fronted him. He had always been that way, and although
still a relatively young man, he was too old to change now.

One man against six heavily-armed hombres who wanted
to kill him wasn't a fight, though—it was suicide. Fargo was

too smart to buck those odds, so when the half-dozen gunnies had spurred out of the brush behind him while he was riding along peacefully and opened fire on him, he did the only sensible thing.

He got the hell out of there.

Unfortunately the men had come after him, still blazing away. Fargo had no idea who they were or why they wanted him dead, but it didn't seem to be the right time and place for asking questions.

The stallion whirled around another bend, momentarily cutting Fargo off from the sight of the rampaging gunmen. He glanced to both right and left in search of some place where he could turn and maybe throw them off his trail, but there was no place to go. The mesquite thickets were virtually impenetrable. Plunging into them would mean that both Fargo and the Ovaro would be clawed to ribbons by the thorny plants.

So all he could do was keep running, no matter how much it went against the grain. Either that or stop and fight it out against overwhelming odds.

Suddenly, as he rounded another bend, another obstacle appeared in front of him. An old man was driving a wagon along the trail, whipping up a team of mules in an attempt to make them go faster. He threw a frantic look over his shoulder as Fargo approached.

Fargo realized that the old-timer must have heard the shooting behind him and wanted to get away, but he had the same problem—there was nowhere to go in this brasada except along the trail. The band of chaparral would end eventually, but too late to do any good for anyone caught in it by the gang of killers.

If those gunmen were willing to cut him down for no apparent reason, Fargo figured they wouldn't spare the old man, either. As he galloped toward the wagon, a plan formed in his head . . . not much of one, but maybe the only chance they would have.

The mules were no match for the Ovaro's speed. Fargo caught up quickly, rode past the wagon, and leaned over to grab the harness on one of the leaders. He reined in and hauled back on the harness with all his considerable strength, turning the mules toward the side of the trail and then bringing them to a halt.

"Dadgum it!" the old-timer on the wagon seat screeched at him. "What the hell do you think you're doin'?"

"Saving our lives, I hope," Fargo told him as he dropped from the stallion's back and pulled his Henry rifle from its saddle sheath. He slapped the Ovaro lightly on the rump and sent the black-and-white horse running around the wagon, which had come to a stop sitting at a slant across the trail.

The back of the wagon held bales of cotton wrapped in jute. That would give Fargo and the old-timer a little shelter from the bullets of the gunmen.

The would-be killers came around the bend and charged toward the wagon. There was no time to waste. Fargo vaulted to the seat, grabbed the old man's stringy arm, and leaped to the ground on the far side of the wagon, pulling the codger along with him. The old-timer yelped in alarm.

"Better pull that hogleg and give me a hand," Fargo said as bullets thudded into the cotton bales and the wooden frame of the wagon. He laid the barrel of the Henry over one of the bales and returned fire, cranking off five shots as fast as he could work the repeater's lever.

Beside him, the old man drew a long-barreled cap-and-ball revolver from a holster at his waist and joined Fargo in firing at their attackers. The heavy roar of the handgun was a sharp contrast to the whipcrack of the rifle.

Like all would-be killers, the gunmen didn't care for it when their intended victims fought back. They reined in as Fargo's slugs and the massive lead balls from the old-timer's pistol began to claw at them. One man swayed in the saddle, dropped his gun, and clapped a hand to his shoulder, which was suddenly bloody where a bullet from the Henry had torn through it.

The wounded gunman managed to stay mounted as the men wheeled their horses and fled. They didn't go far, though, just back around the bend in the trail where they were out of sight from the wagon. As Fargo and the old man held their fire, Fargo heard the hoofbeats stop short, and he had a pretty good idea what the men were up to.

Sure enough, a moment later more shots came from the thorny brush right at the bend. The men had dismounted, crawled back up to where they could draw a bead on the wagon, and opened fire again.

"What'll we do now?" the old-timer asked. "We could send a few howlin' blue whistlers into that brush, but we can't see what we'd be shootin' at!"

"And if you get back on that wagon seat, they'll pick you off," Fargo said. He knew that with the wagon blocking the trail, he could get on the Ovaro and probably make it away safely, shielded by the vehicle, but that would mean abandoning the old man.

Fargo wasn't about to do that. He rose up from behind the cotton bales long enough to throw two shots into the thickets, then ducked down again.

"Looks like we've got a standoff," he said. "Maybe they'll get tired of trying to kill us after a while."

The old man snorted. " 'Tain't likely. Did you see that big jigger in front? That was Johnny Lobo."

Fargo frowned over at the old man as bullets continued to smack into the wagon.

"Yeah, I know it's a damned silly name, but that's what he calls hisself. Since he heads up a bunch o' the most bloodthirsty cutthroats you'll find in these parts, not too many folks make fun of him for it."

Fargo recalled getting a pretty good look at the man the old-timer was talking about. The outlaw leader sat tall and powerful in the saddle, with a barrel chest and a bristling black beard. He'd had a colorful serape draped around his broad shoulders, and the wide-brimmed hat on his head was more piratical than the usual straw or felt sombrero.

"So you don't think this Johnny Lobo will give up and ride away, eh?"

"Especially not after you ventilated one o' his men. He'll want your blood now, for damn sure."

"Why did they open fire on me in the first place? I'm a stranger in these parts."

"Easiest kind to kill and rob." The old man jerked his head toward the Ovaro. "I expect once Johnny caught sight o' that horse o' yours, he wanted it bad. He's got an eye for horseflesh, Johnny does, and that stallion is one fine specimen."

Fargo couldn't argue with that. He and the Ovaro had been together for a lot of years and a lot of miles. The bond between them was more like that between brothers than that of man and horse.

"Well, I don't like it," the old man went on with a sigh, "but I reckon there's only one thing we can do." He took a flask from his pocket, along with flint and steel. "Get ready to jump on that long-legged hoss o' yours and ride, son."

"What are you going to do?" Fargo asked.

"Hide an' watch."

The smell of raw whiskey filled the air as the old man uncorked the flask and doused a corner of one of the cotton bales. He struck a spark, and the whiskey-soaked cotton caught fire with a *whoosh*!

No other series has this much historical action!

THE TRAILSMAN

Available wherever books are sold or at
penguin.com

S310